"I have never been on a horse in my life...

"I've barely even laid eyes on them. How can you expect me to...to ride?"

Emma stood too close to him. He knew she was speaking, but Jonah couldn't concentrate on the words. He liked watching her lips move and had the sudden urge to reach out and crush her to him. To comfort her. To kiss her.

Where did that come from?

Focus, Deardon.

"Stone Creek is only a couple of day's ride from here. I'm sure you're a natural. Besides, we'll stop in one of the town's along the way to rest. You'll be fine," he managed to say.

"Only a couple of day's ri..." Emma threw her hands in the air and walked toward the stairs.

Jonah groaned.

The back of her dress swung back and forth with the gentle sway of her full hips as she moved. He had to change the direction of his thoughts. Now.

"Well, you certainly won't be able to ride in that dress." He cleared his throat.

Emma gasped as she turned and shot him a surprised look.

"And just what is wrong with my dress?" she asked, her hands on her hips.

"Nothing from where I'm standing..."

Also by KELLI ANN MORGAN

THE RANCHER
REDBOURNE SERIES BOOK ONE
COLE'S STORY

THE BOUNTY HUNTER
REDBOURNE SERIES BOOK TWO
RAFE'S STORY

Available from Inspire Books

JONAH

DEARDON MINI-SERIES, BOOK ONE

KELLI ANN MORGAN

inspire books

Inspire Books
A Division of Inspire Creative Services
937 West 1350 North, Clinton, Utah 84015, USA

JONAH

An Inspire Book published by arrangement with the author

First Inspire Books paperback edition August 2013

ISBN-13: 978-1-939049-08-7
ISBN-10: 1939049083

Printed in the United States of America

ACKNOWLEDGEMENTS

To my amazing beta readers, Morgan, Kathy, Camy, and Cheri for giving me four extra sets of eyes. I am lucky to have you!

To my son, Noah, who is so encouraging and excited about my books that he asked me when I would use his name in one of my stories. Needless to say, he is very excited about this series. You are a hero in the making, baby! You don't have to have a book tell you that.

To my amazing formatter, Bob Houston, for always being there when I need you and for saying just the right things to make a girl feel good about herself.

To Jolene Dempster at the St. Joseph Convention and Visitors Bureau in Missouri for spending a good chunk of time working with me on historical details of the city in 1860 and for our enjoyable conversation. You are a delight.

And, as always, to my amazing husband, who is there behind me every step of the way, pushing me to succeed, helping me, encouraging me, and most of all...for loving me. You are my hero!

As always,
To the two biggest heroes in my life,
Grant and Noah,
for a believing in me, loving me,
and sharing me with my characters.

JONAH

DEARDON MINI-SERIES, BOOK ONE

CHAPTER ONE

Boston, September 1860

Marrying someone she'd never met was not on Emma Foster's list of things she had wanted to accomplish in her life, but under the circumstances, she hardly had a choice. Still, the long trek across the country would be arduous.

The train whistle startled her and she nearly dropped her coin purse. It would be so much easier if the train travelled all the way to the Oregon territory, but as it was, at least she would be able to hire someone to take her the rest of the way. She glanced behind her again, unable to shake the feeling that someone was watching her, following her.

"All aboard," the ticket taker called as he leaned from the train car.

Emma put away her satchel, pinched her cheeks, and squared her shoulders. She reached down for the lone travelling case she'd brought for the trip west. With her chin held high, she took the first step up onto the train car.

She looked back at the platform. Couldn't help herself. This may be the last time she would ever see her precious Boston.

With a deep breath and renewed determination, Emma

climbed the last two remaining steps and glanced over the passengers who would accompany her through the first stage of her journey.

People of all shapes and sizes looked back at her—men, women, and children alike. She looked down at the ticket in her hand to locate her seat assignment. As she scanned the aisle, a woman with three unruly children yanking on her skirt and talking to her all at once, met her gaze and smiled. She looked much too young to be their mother, especially to the older looking boy.

Emma mustered a smile of her own and nodded. Of course her seat would be next to them. She closed her eyes and took another deep breath. Gripping the handle of her travelling case tighter, she made her way toward her seat.

"How far are you going?" The young woman asked.

Emma placed her bag on the floor beneath her feet and sat back against the seat. She cleared her throat.

"Oregon."

"You're going to travel that far west all alone?"

Emma turned to look at her new travelling companion and shook her head.

"I'm meeting someone in St. Joseph, Missouri, who'll accompany me the rest of the way."

The last thing she wanted to do was spill her troubles on the first stranger who befriended her. Besides, it was unladylike. Better to keep the tragedy to herself, though she hoped she would make friends in the small Oregon town where she would make her new home with one Mr. Henry Deardon.

Is this really the only way?

Yes, she affirmed.

Emma wanted to believe that she would love the man she married. Her grandfather had not catered to such notions. He'd been a practical man, but Emma hadn't been able to let go of her dream of being swept away by a handsome and wealthy suitor.

"Tickets," the conductor yelled when he stepped into their car.

It took a moment for Emma to realize that her ticket was no longer in her hand. Forcing herself not to panic, she reached down to her travelling case. When she didn't feel the ticket immediately, she retrieved her leather satchel and opened it to look inside.

It wasn't there.

Her breath caught in her chest and she turned quickly from side to side, searching the floor and the surrounding area of her seat.

After a few moments, she stopped, sat upright, and recounted each movement she'd made since she'd boarded the train. The ticket should be in her hand. It wasn't long before the mischievous giggle of the women's children reached her ears. They had been playing on the heavy wooden crates behind the seat. She narrowed her eyes, then whipped around to look at them.

When the boy, obviously the eldest of the children, caught her stare, he elbowed the girl next to him, sat up straight, and tried to wipe the smirk from his face. The girl quickly shoved her hands beneath her bottom, but not before Emma saw the object of their amusement. Her ticket.

She glanced over at the young woman next to her whose arms were folded, a soft peaceful expression on her face. Emma did not understand how she could look so calm. These children were rambunctious to say the least, yet she seemed unperturbed by them.

Emma wasn't particularly fond of children and this just confirmed her reasoning. They were messy and loud, and well, the truth was, she'd never really been around them. Her time had been spent mostly on lessons in arithmetic, music, and grammar. Livvy, her governess, had always told her she had an old soul.

Emma had half a mind to turn around and lift the little girl by her ankles to shake the ticket loose, but thought better of it. The children would probably just find the gesture amusing. No, this was going to be a long ride and she didn't desire to spend it in a constant dance with these miniature hooligans.

The ticket taker was getting closer.

Emma turned around and locked stares with the young girl in braids, who opened her eyes wide with feigned innocence. The temptation to turn the child upside down grew, but instead she leaned into the woman next to her.

"Excuse me," Emma said.

"Yes?"

How could she say this without upsetting her? Maybe she would just pretend ignorance. "I seem to have lost my ticket, just in the time since I've sat down. Have you seen it?"

The woman raised an eyebrow and patted Emma on the leg. "Just one moment," she said before standing up.

A man sitting on the next row saw her stand up. He lifted himself from his seat, but the young woman shook her head and patted the air in front of her. He sat back down with a slight nod and returned to the book he'd been reading a moment before.

Turning to look at the children, the woman simply held out her hand and waited.

Emma glanced back and forth between them. When the young girl pulled the ticket from beneath her and passed it forward, Emma's jaw nearly dropped.

It worked.

A string of giggles erupted behind her.

"There you are." The young woman placed the ticket in Emma's hand. "I'm sorry about that. Sometimes they get it in their minds to play tricks on people."

Emma forced a smile at the children.

Relief washed over her. When the uniformed man held out his hand expectantly for the ticket, she held it up. He punched it and moved to the next row.

"No harm done," she said and exhaled loudly.

Emma opened her satchel, carefully placed the ticket inside, and set the bag on top of her luggage—aside her feet.

"Your children are rather…spirited," Emma said with a grin. Although she hated to admit it, their playful manner had endeared them to her. A little.

"They are spirited, but just how old do you think I am?"

Emma's eyes widened. "I…" She didn't know what to say.

"Johnny is near thirteen. He and his little sister, Callie," she pointed her chin at the youngest of the children, "lost their parents near six months ago and the orphanage here just doesn't have room. Fran there," she pointed at the child with long blond braids who'd taken Emma's ticket, "is what we call a runner. She just won't stay where she's put."

Emma faced forward and flattened her back against her seat to absorb the information she'd just obtained.

Orphans? She looked back at the young woman and scrunched her eyebrows together.

"We're headed to Kansas to join the Orphan Train. We hope to find all of them good homes. However, at least for now, they are my responsibility. I'm Hattie by the way."

Emma had never met another orphan before. She risked a quick glance behind her at the faces of the children. She'd lost her parents when she'd been just three years old, but she'd had her grandfather to take care of her. She wondered what could have happened to her if he hadn't been there.

When he died…

Well, she didn't want to think about that right now.

"It's a pleasure to meet you, Hattie. I'm Emma," she said with a nod.

"Emma," Hattie confirmed. "What is taking you out west?"

Emma shifted in her seat enough that her neck wasn't straining to look at Hattie. Suddenly, the hairs on the back of her neck stood on edge and she quickly glanced over the car for any familiar faces.

No one.

Emma exhaled slowly, returning her focus to Hattie, and started a condensed version of her little story.

"My inheritance."

CHAPTER TWO

Oregon, Three Weeks Earlier

"Henry agreed to marry the girl, not me." Jonah Deardon paced the room.

It had only been three days since they'd buried his older brother. As if the grief wasn't enough, now his father was intent on pawning Henry's poor decisions off on him. He'd loved his brother, but they had rarely seen eye to eye on anything of importance.

A bride.

Jonah shook his head.

"We have an agreement with Mr. Foster. And Deardon's do not go back on their word." His father stood up from his desk and pounded his fists against the flat wood.

Jonah threw his hands through his hair.

"And making rash promises on a whim is exactly why we are in this predicament in the first place." He knew it wasn't fair to bring it up, and he regretted the words as soon as they'd left his mouth.

His father looked down, his arms locked, still bracing him on the desk with closed fists.

It had been nearly fifteen years since Jonah had seen his

grandparents. Gabe Deardon was a stubborn man and when he'd vowed to keep his sons away from his father over a stupid argument, he'd turned his back on everything the Deardon fortune offered him—family, wealth, freedom, opportunity. And for what? To keep his pride?

Well, Jonah wasn't his father. Freedom and opportunity were very high on his list, and getting married now would take that all away. It seemed women only made a mess of things and he was in no hurry to saddle himself to one.

After a few seconds, his father lifted his head and looked at him, his brows crumpled with concern.

Marriage was not in Jonah's immediate plans, especially to a young, spoiled society girl from some place back East. No, there had to be another way to keep the land they'd worked so hard to cultivate—and his freedom.

Still silence.

"Jonah?" his father finally spoke, but with a resigned quiet in his voice that Jonah hadn't expected.

He couldn't meet his father's eyes.

A soft whinny carried on the slight breeze through the open window.

"Father, we are already behind schedule. And without Henry..." his voice trailed at the sadness that accompanied the realization of his words.

Henry had never been scared of anything—even when he should have been. This drive was going to be hard enough, but without him Jonah wasn't sure how they'd manage.

"These horses have to be delivered to the Pony Express stations within a fortnight as promised or we'll lose the contract," Jonah said matter-of-factly. He crossed the room and opened the front door, then paused without looking back. "I'll think about it."

Before he could pull the door shut behind him, Gabe Deardon made up the distance between him and his second son and placed a booted foot in its path.

"We'll get through this, son." He placed a hand on Jonah's shoulder. "We always do. Just remember what we've built here, Jonah. Keeping the ranch depends on more than fulfilling our contract with the Pony Express. It depends on retaining this land. Miss Foster is the key to that."

Jonah met his father's gaze without a word, turned on his heel, and headed to the corral. This drive would provide the time he needed to figure things out. There had to be a way to satisfy both sides without getting hitched in the process and he was going to find it.

"Where are we on finding another drover, Maxie?" he asked the man leaning against the corral fence with a long piece of wheat-colored grass protruding from his mouth.

Max pushed himself away from the fence and fell in step with Jonah as they circled the barn. "Sent one of the boys to the logging camp up river. Eli Whittaker has been the only other volunteer so far," he said with a smirk.

Jonah jerked around to look at his longtime friend and best drover. "The kid's barely twelve years old and scrawny as hell."

"Just telling what we got, boss."

Jonah narrowed his eyes at the unvoiced chuckle he knew was hovering just beneath the surface of Max's serious façade and snorted. "We're losing daylight standing around here. This mob needs to be ready to ride first thing tomorrow." He grabbed his gloves from the small milking stool outside the stable and threw open the doors.

Maybe a ride would do him some good. Clear his head. Then, he thought about the long hours he'd have ahead in the saddle and thought better of it. He needed three horses for each of the selected Pony Express stations along the route between Salt Lake City and St. Joseph, Missouri. That meant delivering nearly one-hundred and fifty horses short one very experienced wrangler. It could be done. It would have to be.

"What bee crawled into your bonnet tonight?" Max threw the grass he'd been chewing to the ground, followed Jonah into the stable, and climbed up onto the rung of one of the stall gates.

Jonah shoved his hands through his hair and kicked at a small rock in the dirt. Glass shattered as it pierced the outer casing of the lantern on the work table.

"Damn."

"Feel better?" Lucas Deardon, Jonah's baby brother, leaned against the stable door and folded his arms.

"Why don't you or Noah marry the girl? An ugly, no good scoundrel like yourself may never get another chance," Jonah teased, trying to lighten his own mood.

His younger brothers, Noah and Lucas, were in no short supply of female attentions. And if he were honest with himself, there were a few gals in town that had not been too subtle about letting him know where he could hang his hat either.

"Not every woman is going to be like mama," Lucas said out of nowhere.

Jonah didn't want to think about the woman who'd abandoned her husband and four small boys thirteen years earlier because a fancy easterner had told her that a voice like hers deserved to been heard from a big city stage. She'd left for Chicago within the week. Jonah had been eleven years old, but Lucas had only been seven.

A loud boom nearly shook the ground and a streak of lightning split the sky.

"When is Aunt Leah expecting us at Redbourne Ranch for the wedding?" Noah ducked into the stable just as the clouds broke and the rain started to fall.

Jonah threw his hands in the air and walked out into the rain.

"What? What did I say?"

Jonah heard Noah's question through the onslaught of water that slammed against his hat and dripped down the rim in surprisingly thick cascades. He'd sent word to Kansas of Henry's accident just this morning, but with the way mail was handled, who knew how long it would be before they received word?

"You don't have to marry her, you know." Lucas patted him firmly on the shoulder.

"Tell that to him." Jonah nodded his head toward the back door, where their father leaned against the frame with his coffee mug in hand.

The original plan had been to retrieve Miss Foster in St. Joseph and then head down to Stone Creek, Kansas where she and Henry would be wed at Redbourne Ranch. It would have all worked out fine, but Henry had to go and get himself killed and that changed everything.

Now, with just five weeks left, he had no idea if Miss Foster would receive his letter, let alone Aunt Leah. He couldn't just leave a woman stranded. They were less than a week behind schedule, but that could be a lifetime if Emma Foster was waiting for Henry in St. Joseph, Missouri.

What was he going to say if and when he found her? Could he actually marry the girl to save his family's ranch? Truth was, they'd collected about all the free land surrounding the ranch they could, but the Foster's property claimed the pass, the best grazing land for miles, and the biggest source of water. They needed this parcel. There was no denying it.

Ezra, the old cook, stepped out onto the disheveled porch of the bunkhouse and clanked the metal triangle with his steel stick.

"Come on, boys," Noah called as he pushed past Jonah and Lucas, "supper's on," he said with a laugh, attempting to block his uncovered head from the rain with his arms.

Jonah glanced back up at the front door.

His father was gone.

He pulled his hat down tighter on his head and put his arm around his brother.

"Let the drive begin."

CHAPTER THREE

St. Joseph, Missouri

"I'll take those, ma'am," Johnny called from the bottom of the train steps.

Emma smiled at how she'd warmed to the orphan children and their caretaker on their journey west.

"Why, thank you, kind sir," she said in an exaggeratedly demure drawl as she handed her travelling case down.

Johnny rolled his eyes, but Emma didn't miss the pink color that darkened his cheeks. A touch of melancholy set in as she realized this was where they would all part ways. She took a step down, but before she could reach the bottom, Johnny had raised a hand to help her.

Emma placed her fingers in his palm and when she attained the platform, she bowed her head with a slight curtsy.

"Why, Johnny Dingle, if I didn't know any better I would say you was whooped over Miss Foster," Fran teased, her hands on her hips and braids swinging around her shoulders.

His smile froze in place and a deeper color flooded his face. "Ma'am." He tipped an imaginary hat toward her and turned on his heel.

Fran's eyes widened when he barreled straight toward her.

Emma laughed.

"You sure you have to do this?" Hattie asked. "Oregon is awfully far, and for a man you've never even met." She tsked.

Emma looked at her new friend and didn't want to admit the truth. That her grandfather had taught her to be a lady with finer skills and attributes. She had no idea how to wash clothes, care for children, or keep a house. And the only other jobs for a woman were…unthinkable at best. She shook her head of the dreadful thoughts and smiled.

"My grandfather knew what he was doing when he made this arrangement. I am sure that Mr. Deardon will take good care of me." She glanced around from one end of the platform to the other, but it seemed no one was here waiting for her.

She would not panic.

I'm sure he has just been delayed, she thought.

When Emma realized that Hattie was looking at her with creased brows, she smiled as warmly as she could and leaned down to hug the woman.

A little tug on her skirt drew her attention.

"Don't go, Emma. I mean, Miss Foster. I want you to be our new mommy." The child's wide blue eyes brimmed with tears. "I think Johnny would like that too."

Hattie laughed loudly and winked at Emma. She picked up the little girl. "Now, Callie, Miss Emma is going west to get married. Don't you worry, we'll find you and your brother a good family."

Callie reached for Emma, but Hattie held her tight.

Emma stepped forward and placed a hand over the little girl's and leaned in close to the child's face. "But we'll be great friends always, all right?" she whispered.

Callie nodded with a sniffle and Hattie set her down. The

child remained still for a moment, not quite able to meet Emma's eyes, but then, with a quick glance, she spun on her heel and ran to her brother, clasping him about his leg and tucking her head into the folds of his shirt. Johnny put his arm around his little sister and with a half-smile, squeezed her closer.

Emma had never really thought about children, but there was a slight tug to her heart as she stepped back and stood up straight.

"It's time to go." The deep, resonating voice of the man with the book from the train startled her. He'd appeared out of nowhere. "They are waiting for us at the new St. Joseph's church."

Hattie and Emma exchanged glances.

"Goodbye, my friend," Hattie said with another quick hug. "And God speed."

The hairs on Emma's neck bristled again. Her head shot up, her eyes scanning the boardwalk. Most of the passengers had already made their way off the platform. A gangly man in a fashionable brown suit pulled a pocket watch from his vest. He twitched his nose, moving his spectacles higher, and shook his head.

An older woman ushered two young girls toward the station's entrance and the train's ticket taker stood to the side of the train carriage with his hands behind his back. There was no sign of anyone she thought could be Henry Deardon.

Emma looked at the large clock looming over the door of the covered area of the platform. Four o'clock. Surely he hadn't left her over being half an hour later than expected.

She spotted an empty bench on the landing just down a few steps on the far side of the station and reached for her travel bags. But when she lifted the large carrying case, the handle gave way and it dropped heavily back to the ground. She looked heavenward and closed her eyes.

Give me strength, she pleaded silently.

Luckily, the latch holding the bag together held firm and her belongings did not scatter across the train platform. She tucked her satchel beneath her arm and bent down in attempt to lift the monstrosity from the bottom.

"Looks like you're needing some help there, little lady."

Emma looked up to see a tall, fairly robust man with a shiny badge gleaming from outside the pocket of his vest.

"Why, yes, deputy. Thank you."

"Where ya headed?"

"Oregon."

He choked on a laugh that stumbled from his throat.

Emma giggled nervously.

The prickly feeling returned. She had been unable to rid herself of the feeling someone was watching her. Maybe the man she was intended to meet here and marry was observing her from afar, testing her somehow. She glanced around again.

No one.

"I'm sorry. I'm looking for Mr. Henry Deardon. He was supposed to meet me here at half past three and I'm afraid I do not see him."

"Deardon, huh?" The deputy scratched the whiskers on his chin with the back of his hand. "Cain't say I know any Henry Deardon. Is he from around these parts?"

It was a long story and Emma really didn't want to explain it to the man.

"I think I'll wait a while? I am sure he will be here to retrieve me shortly."

The deputy nodded, picked up her bag, and together they walked right past the bench around to the front of the large, red brick railroad depot. Carriages and wagons lined the front walk. The deputy wasn't much for small talk and she found herself nearly running to keep up with his long strides.

"Much more to see of our beautiful town on this side of the depot." The deputy nodded at her again with a wink and a smile. He set her travelling case down at the foot of an iron bench resting against one of the three oversized brick arches that made up the front entrance to the station. "Most folks that stop by the station come in through here. Besides, I'll feel better about you waiting alone if I can keep an eye on ya."

"Thank you, deputy…"

"Jarvis, ma'am. You can just call me Jarvis."

"Thank you…Jarvis."

He tipped his hat and walked across the overly wide street toward a small collection of buildings and what appeared to be the jailhouse. The tall structures framing the boardwalk from the street behind them reminded Emma a little of home. Though, in reality, they were nothing compared to the towering edifices of Boston.

Her stomach grumbled. It had been hours since she'd had something to eat and the last of the dried fruit Livvy had packed for her had long since been devoured.

Emma sat down on the bench and opened her satchel. She glanced up and looked around to make sure no one was watching her and she pulled her coin purse from the bag. A few dollar bills remained, but mostly she had coins. There was not enough for a return ticket to Boston, although she knew she had nothing to go back to even if there were.

She took a deep breath.

The sun fell down behind the buildings. Emma had no idea how long she had been waiting there, but she'd sat, stood, and paced for what had seemed like an eternity waiting for her soon-to-be husband and had had quite a long time to think about what she would do if he didn't show.

Staying on the bench all night was certainly not an option. Emma leaned her elbows against her knees and rested her chin in her hands.

A woman, clad in a blue gingham dress, sauntered across the street toward her.

Emma lifted her head, straightened her back, and quickly brushed at the unsightly crinkles in her new lavender travelling dress. She stood.

"Hello," the woman said, pushing up the sleeves on her arms. She bent down and picked up the whole travelling case, turned, and started to walk away.

Emma's mouth dropped wide open and she stared in disbelief.

Midway through the street, the odd woman turned back to look over her shoulder. "We're about to have some supper. You comin'?"

Emma was speechless. At first, she didn't move, then her stomach made a noise that she was near positive it had never made in her life. She quickly looked about. There was nothing else to grab but her satchel, which she snatched up into her hands. Then, she pinched her cheeks and hurriedly fell in step behind the kindly lady, a slight smile touching her lips.

When she reached the cobblestone half-wall with stairs that separated the street from the yard, she paused to look at the newly whitewashed two-story home with its quaint little railed porch and abundance of windows. The front door snapped shut behind the woman and Emma thought it would be best to get inside. Everything she owned was inside that travelling case and it would serve her well to keep it in her sights.

The warm and distinct scent of chicken and biscuits filled her nostrils and she closed her eyes to the welcoming aroma. Her mouth began to water and her stomach protested even louder than before.

"Come in, young'n and have a seat with the rest of us."

Emma walked into the entry way, wiped her feet on the red woven rug, and followed the woman around a corner to where a near dozen assortment of people were already seated at a large candlelit table, including Jarvis.

"Ma'am," he said with a nod and removed his hat.

Emma bit her bottom lip.

"I realize you're waitin' for your fella, but it looks like he may not make it tonight. I can't leave ya sittin' on that bench outside all night, so have yourself a seat and get some vittles in your belly."

Emma unpinned her own hat, placed it on the large wooden chest to her left, and joined the rest of them at the table.

"Thank you, um…" she trailed when she realized she had not even gotten the woman's name.

"Millie," she provided. "And you're welcome."

Grace was said.

"Now, tell us what's taking you to Oregon."

CHAPTER FOUR

Three Days Later

Jonah had left Noah and Lucas back at the Pony Express stables. Most of the rest of the crew he'd paid in advance and when they'd hit the Nebraska territory, he'd stocked up Ezra's wagon and sent those men back for home. He'd kept on a few drovers to aid them in the last leg of the journey, but by the time they'd reached St. Joseph, they were down to a mere twenty head or so. The men and the horses deserved a break. They'd ridden hard to make the journey in record time.

The Patee House hotel was the headquarters for the Pony Express and Jonah hoped he would find Mr. Russell, the benefactor of this drive, there. Jonah had never been comfortable around people with obvious wealth and the Patee House was exactly the kind of hotel that attracted those of affluence. He preferred the smaller inns and boarding houses that came with a nice home cooked meal and oft times a hot shave.

While he waited, he watched city folk walk in and out of the lobby with their fancy luggage and duds. He shifted his weight and leaned back against the wall, all but out of sight.

Yes, the sooner he collected their payment and left, the better. When he spotted a young man in denims, a button down shirt, and a brown leather vest walking across the vast lobby area with purpose—the kid's hair amuck and face lined in smudges—Jonah guessed him to be one of the famed Pony Express Riders. Hit hat went off to the kid. He'd have signed up for that kind of adventure himself, but with his size and stature, they would have just laughed at him.

After forty-five minutes, Mr. Russell met with him in his bottom floor office, looked over his books with all the delivery signatures, and paid him in full. Jonah was on the way out the door, when he stopped at the front desk. A short, thin gentleman with a thick, but waxed mustache greeted him.

"May I be of assistance?" he asked with a tilt of his head. His collar looked much too tight.

Jonah cleared his throat. "I am looking for a woman who may be a guest of yours. Do you have an Emma Foster staying here?"

The clerk glanced down at his rather large, ledger looking book, and scanned the page in front of him. "I'm afraid there is no one by that name."

Damn.

Miss Foster had not been waiting at the train station when they'd arrived in town. It was no surprise. What had he expected her to do? A lady in her position was sure to have found a grand hotel to stay in. Maybe she'd received his post and hadn't made the trip after all. His hope felt empty somehow.

"Do you have a telegraph office in town?" He figured he'd better find out for sure before heading out.

"Yes, sir. You'll find it just over on Sixth, directly across from the train depot."

"Thank you." Jonah tipped his hat at the man and walked out to the hitching post at the bottom of the stairs where he'd tied Perseus, his horse, and climbed up without acknowledging any of the passersby. With the amount of money now tucked in his jacket, the last thing he needed was to call a lot of attention to himself.

The tall buildings that rose up on either side of him as he rode the six blocks to the stables reminded him how grateful he was to have the trees and open land that surrounded the Deardon spread. There was no freedom to be found in a big city and he itched to get on his way. He half expected the crew to be lounged about and sleeping when he returned to the Pony Express stables, but when he arrived, the men were all standing out back hooting and hollering at Lucas who was entertaining them with some of the tricks he'd learned from a ridiculous cowboy working with some rodeo circus nonsense earlier in the year.

Jonah shook his head and dismounted.

"Did you find your bride?" Noah teased when Jonah joined his brother on the outer fence.

"Nope."

Jonah looked up when the men all gasped. Lucas was lying on the ground, his horse still running circles around the enclosed yard. Jonah's heart seemed to jump from his chest and emotions all too fresh washed over him. He ran to the shorter gate and sprang over the top without so much as a thought.

When Lucas sat up and started to brush off the stray pieces of grass that had collected on his shirt, Jonah breathed a quick sigh of relief before pulling his brother to his feet. He wanted to yell. Wanted to knock some sense into his brother. Instead, he grabbed him and pulled him into a fierce hug.

"Sorry, Jonah. I wasn't thinking."

Jonah squeezed him tighter and then let him go with a shove, walking away before Lucas could see the pool of tears that had accumulated on the rims of his lids. Henry had been so sure he could ride the rogue mustang. It had been a fool way to die, and Jonah would be damned if he would let it happen to another of his brothers.

It was time to get these men paid and find the idiot woman who'd agreed to marry a man she'd never even met. Aunt Leah would be expecting them.

"Just what exactly do I do with that?" Emma asked, her nose upturned, staring out of the corner of her eye at the rather large pile of horse dung steaming near the front gate of the rooming house.

Millie had been gracious enough to let Emma help around the house to pay for her room and board, but the woman just couldn't afford to hire on someone new, especially someone who had to be taught how to complete even the simplest of housekeeping tasks.

"Oh, don't you pay no nevermind, child. Old Jed McIntire is bringing the last of his crop to sell at the edge of town today and we'll be needing some fresh goods. Best get there early on to get the best of it. Go collect your shawl and a basket."

Not waiting for Millie to change her mind, Emma skittered up the stairs and into the house without a word. She leaned briefly against the closed door and darted to the small room behind the kitchen where she'd been sleeping, and opted for her lighter fabric shawl. She retrieved her small coin purse from her satchel, then picked up a worn handled over-sized basket from the edge of the kitchen counter.

It would be nice to get out for a stroll. It would give her time to think of how she might be able to earn the money for a train ticket to…

To where exactly?

How had she been such a fool to believe that everything would work out? Her grandfather had always told her that everything happened for a reason, but the reason she would be stranded in this town near penniless and without a husband escaped her.

When she reached the bottom of the last set of stone steps in the yard, the muck was gone. Millie handed her some coins and a list she'd scribbled down on an old yellowed scratch of paper.

"Now, get on with ya," Millie said with a smirk. "We'll be needing some fresh corn and apples for tonight's supper."

Emma looked down at the change and wondered where the woman had been carrying her money. It was probably best she didn't know. She placed the coins in her small purse and rushed down the boardwalk toward the edge of town where the farmer would be selling his goods.

When Emma had finished collecting everything on her list, she neatly tucked the paper in her little purse and set it atop the basket sitting at her feet when she felt the hairs of her neck stand on end. She quickly glanced about her. No one seemed to be paying any particular attention to her, and then she saw him. A man *had* been watching her, but before she'd been able to fix on his features, he'd ducked behind an oncoming wagon and disappeared.

Emma suddenly felt on edge. There had been something familiar about the figure, but she couldn't place it. She bent down to pick up the now heavy basket and realized that with the large load, the handles wouldn't hold.

"The rider is coming!" someone shouted from the next street over.

Rider?

The woman standing next to her, grabbed her skirts and lifted, running toward the street corner and knocking Emma off balance in the process. Men and women, who moments ago had been busy looking over the wares of the old farmer and his wife, as well as others who had been making their way casually down the street, all rushed to the edge of the road and strained their necks to peer at what Emma assumed was a Pony Express rider. Jarvis had regaled them all with tales of the brave young men who ventured across country to deliver mail.

Cheers could be heard in waves as the rider approached. When Emma finally caught sight of him, she was surprised to see a young man, no older than young Johnny from the train, whisking past the crowd. While his head was focused on the road ahead, he still managed a swift wave of his hand to the onlookers. It wasn't long before dust filled the street and the rider all but disappeared.

In moments, the crowd began to disperse and return to their previous activities. The food stuffs in Emma's basket overflowed, but finally she managed to wrap her arms fully around the bulging frame. She turned back awkwardly toward the rooming house.

Thud. The basket was knocked free of her grasp in an instant and the three plump tomatoes that had lined the top had been squished into her chest.

She was ready to 'spit nails' as Jarvis would say. She looked up to tell the dolt who'd just run into her what she thought of his lumbering attack, when she was met by the most beautiful rich brown eyes she'd ever seen.

He reached into his pocket and retrieved a handkerchief, which he motioned forward toward her now sopping chest. He must have thought better of it because his hands twitched, unknowing how to proceed.

Good heavens, he was going to try to wipe the tomatoes from her bosom. Heat immediately rushed into her face and she took a small step backward.

"Excuse me, ma'am," he said with a voice that would

melt butter. After positioning his hands a few different ways, he tossed his handkerchief onto her chest and color immediately stained his cheeks. "Um, here, take this."

She didn't recall a time when she'd seen such a handsome man so flustered. In fact, she didn't recall when she'd seen such a handsome man.

He opened his mouth to speak, then closed it. After looking everywhere but at her, he tipped his hat, the wide berth of which she'd never seen before, and turned away.

"I'm sorry," he called out as he retreated down the road.

He's leaving?

She looked at the mess of food scattered about the road. A small group of poorly dressed youth ran past her and kicked some of the potatoes from her reach.

Of all the—

"Excuse my brother, ma'am," a blond gentleman said, scooping up some of the wayward potatoes. "Jonah's in a bit of a hurry chasing after the woman he thinks may be his unsuspecting betrothed," he continued, collecting a few more items from the road.

"No wonder she's running away from him," she started, putting a few ears of corn into the grounded basket, "with manners like those." She nearly choked on her words when she glanced up and saw the dashing smile that lit the man's tanned and chiseled features. It really was unfair that one family could be blessed with such looks.

The stranger chortled. "Let me help you with that." He bent down and picked up her basket. "You headed far?"

"Noah, look at this," another man approached. "They have cantaloupe and watermelon. It's been a long time."

Three of them?

"Are there any more of you?"

Noah laughed.

The new stranger looked down, seeming to notice her for

the first time. "Well, hello. Aren't you a lady fit for a man's arm? I'm Lucas," he said with a smile.

Emma couldn't help her but smile at the sight of him bowing with a melon in each arm.

"It's just the three of us now," Noah answered her question. "We lost our oldest brother last month in an accident while trying to break a mustang."

"Oh, my," Emma gasped, "I'm so sorry to hear that. You must be devastated."

"It was tough. Still is, but I think it hit Jonah the hardest." He looked back at the place where his brother had disappeared from sight. "Come on, now. That's enough about that. Where are we going with this mighty fine basket of goods?"

Emma took a step in the direction she'd come. She'd never had such fine gentlemanly attention. She liked it.

"I'm just down the road at the boarding house. The owner was gracious enough to let me stay at her place while I…make some decisions."

"You're staying at Millie's?" Lucas asked, falling in step with her and Noah.

Emma nodded.

"Now, that's a mighty fine coincidence." Lucas held out an arm to her. "We're headed there ourselves."

"Thank you, Mr. Lucas." Emma placed her hand on his forearm. "Thank you both for your kind assistance."

"Oh, it's not *Mr.* Lucas. Just Lucas. Deardon."

Deardon?

"Oh, my."

CHAPTER FIVE

Besides the new Patee House, there were four other hotels in town. Miss Foster had to be staying in one of them. Jonah'd had a mind just to travel down to Redbourne Ranch without her, but thought twice when he imagined the look he would be sure to see on Aunt Leah's face when he told her they were short a bride.

He'd almost resigned himself to the idea of marrying her solely for the good of the family when he accidentally bumped into the most beautiful woman he'd ever laid eyes on. Her ebony hair was a stark contrast against eyes that were a most rare muted blue and looked like they'd been filled with the morning's mist.

When he realized that he'd caused her tomatoes to be squished into the bodice of her dress, he pulled his handkerchief from his pocket and stepped toward her to help clean the mess. It didn't take long for him to realize that it wasn't going to work and he simply tossed the cloth at her. He had to stop dwelling on the perfect swell of her bosom and needed to refocus his thoughts on finding Emma Foster and convincing her not to marry him.

Jonah looked up and met Noah's eyes. His brothers had

been following fairly close behind him and Noah, at least, had
seen the incident. His brother nodded and stopped to help
the woman with the food basket, or what was left of it. Guilt
settled in his gut, but Jonah took comfort in knowing that
Noah would help the young woman and hopefully settle any
damages.

No, he wasn't ready to give up on marrying someone of
his own choosing. Not yet.

Maybe when he found Miss Foster, he could convince
her of an alternate arrangement. Just what that arrangement
would be hadn't occurred to him yet, but there had to be a
way to come to a new agreement without getting married.
Surely she would see reason.

More than once today he'd seen a young woman
travelling alone with a bag in hand and had stopped her to
inquire her name. None reported to be Emma Foster from
Boston, including this last young lady.

"I'm staying at the Patee House…just in case you don't
find her," the woman told him with a coy smile.

Jonah didn't remember the women in his life being so
bold. Yet another reason he did not appreciate big cities. How
he was going to find the woman in a town this size was
beyond him, if she was even here. What if she'd received his
post and he'd wasted all morning looking for her for nothing?

"Thank you kindly for your time, ma'am," Jonah said,
turning and walking back toward the boarding house he and
his brothers had booked for the night.

He needed to get a message to the Foster house in
Boston and was grateful the telegraph office was on the way
to Millie's place. He was confident that he would be able to
get a response within the day. If only the telegraph line
already extended across the continent, he wouldn't be in this
mess. It would sure beat this guess work he was doing.

As Jonah passed the spot where he'd knocked into the

young woman with her groceries, he was disappointed to see that the mess had all been cleaned up, and she was nowhere to be seen. His brothers would have helped her along and then headed back to the house.

He tried to determine what it was about her that had captivated him and couldn't decide on just one thing. There had been something about her that he had connected with—something in her eyes that had spoken to him.

Enough.

Jonah had his hands full trying to find one woman. Looking for two seemed out of the question, but there had been something in her eyes—those wide, innocent eyes—that had touched him.

A glint caught his eye and he glanced down. There in the road, peeking out from beneath a discarded corn husk, was a small coin purse.

It can't be.

He picked it up and closed his fingers over his discovery. A little hope never hurt anyone. He smiled and made his way over to the telegraph office.

"I need you to send this message to Boston," Jonah said the moment he stepped into the quaint building with barely enough standing room to breathe. He slid the paper with a brief scribbled message and location across the counter.

The clerk sitting behind the desk brushed stray crumbs from his mustache and cleared his throat. He stood and picked up the note.

"Boston, huh?" he asked picking something from his teeth with his tongue.

Jonah didn't say anything, he just waited.

The operator sat down on a tall stool just in front of the black machine on an elevated table. He placed spectacles over his eyes and held Jonah's note between his fingertips as he leaned onto the table and began to hit the keys in rhythm.

Jonah was fascinated. He'd heard about the practice multiple times, but he'd never actually seen it. He leaned back against the wall nonchalantly, but watched closely through the corner of his eye. He perked up his head when beeping sounds came in reply.

"They've received it, but it won't be delivered to the Foster residence until morning." The telegraph operator leaned up onto his stool. "So, now we wait."

Jonah pushed himself off the wall. "I'm late for supper. When something comes in, will you have it delivered to Millie's place?"

"You're staying with Miss Millie?" the clerk asked with wide eyes and a barely contained grin.

Jonah nodded.

"I'll bring it over myself," he said and jumped off his stool with an outstretched hand, which Jonah shook firmly.

"I'll be waiting."

When Jonah walked through the front door of the boarding house, the welcoming warmth of freshly baked bread and hot butter greeted him. His mouth started to water instantly. He'd been unaware of just how hungry he'd been. The idea of eating something other than Ezra's watered down vegetable stew pushed him to move quickly. They'd only stayed at Millie's place once before, after delivery of their first small herd to the Pony Express, but if memory served him correctly, the food had been better than anything he'd ever eaten. They deserved it after the trip they'd had.

It'd been a long journey from Oregon to Missouri and he was looking forward to a warm meal, a hot bath and shave, and a good night's sleep. That is, if thoughts of a certain young woman's muted blue eyes would stop haunting him.

Jonah quickly hung his hat on the rack behind the door. He pulled the pocket watch from his vest. Supper had most certainly already been served and he was not about to miss the meal. He tossed the little coin purse in the air and caught it again, whistling his way to the dining room.

When he walked around the corner, he was met by a half dozen sets of eyes. He stopped his tune with a smirk.

"Jonah," Noah said from the far end of the table, "come join us. We have so much to tell you."

Immediately, Jonah was put on edge. Something was amiss. Noah's grin spread from ear to ear and he looked as if he were about to trap Jonah into doing something he wouldn't want to do. He raised an eyebrow and slowly made his way to the empty chair next to his brother.

"What have you done now?" Jonah asked speculatively, pulling the chair out far enough for him to sit.

Most people would call Millie's dining area small, but she liked to say it was just a cozy place for folks to get to know one another. He sat down, still looking at his brother.

"Jonah, I would like you to meet Emma Foster."

Jonah's expression froze on his face. He didn't dare look. Thoughts raced through his head. What was he going to say? What was he going to do? He closed his eyes and in that instant, his head had betrayed him by turning toward the surprise dinner guest. When he opened his eyes again, he had to blink a few times before he realized that the eyes that had been haunting him all day stared back at him. His jaw dropped.

Noah elbowed him sharply in the ribs. Jonah grunted and hunched over in his chair, one forearm catching on the edge of the table. It took a moment to recover, but when he finally was able to look up, he managed a smile. He lifted a hand to tip his hat and realized that he'd hung the damn thing on the rack when he'd first come in.

Emma was unimpressed. He could tell from the stoic expression on her face. Her arms were folded and her back was nearly as straight as the chair.

Millie pushed her seat back and all three brothers stood up. From the color staining Millie's cheeks, Jonah could see she was pleased.

"Now, why don't you gentlemen just sit yourselves down and finish eating your food. Mr. Deardon," she turned her attention to Jonah, "dish yourself up some of these fixin's and I'll be back momentarily with more mashed potatoes and gravy."

"Thanks, *Miss Berkshire*," Jonah said with a smile.

"I told you to call me Mill…ah." She nodded her head. "I'll be back with those potatoes, *Jonah*."

All three brothers laughed.

Jonah dared a glance at Emma.

The corners of her mouth twitched and she quickly folded her lips together. She reached for a glass of water and after taking a small sip, she returned the glass to the table and glanced up at him.

He could feel his brothers watching him. His fingers played with the small latch on the top of the coin purse he held.

The coin purse.

"Miss," he cleared his throat, "Foster?"

She continued to stare at him—her expression not unpleasant.

"I believe you may have dropped this in the street when I so rudely bumped into you earlier today." He swallowed.

Emma's eyes grew wide and she placed a hand over her open mouth. "I didn't even know I'd lost it." As if afraid he might bite her, she slowly reached out across the table to his hand holding her small bag.

When her fingers grazed his palm, he closed his hand over hers and she gasped a little.

"Please excuse my abrupt departure. I hope Noah and Lucas saw to it that you had everything you needed."

Her eyelashes quickly fluttered against her newly stained cheeks.

"Thank you. They were perfect gentlemen."

He let go, but didn't miss the soft smile that now graced her beautiful features. Maybe getting married wasn't going to be such a bad thing after all.

CHAPTER SIX

Emma sucked in a breath when Jonah Deardon grasped her hand in his. That little coin purse contained all the money she still had to her name within its confines. His touch warmed her, though thoughts of decorum screamed at the impropriety of holding a man's hand, let alone a stranger's. She couldn't make herself pull away.

After he apologized for his behavior in the street and for abandoning her to the mercy of his brothers, she could no longer feign indifference. He released her hand and she drew her coin purse into her lap.

Emma looked up to meet Jonah's eyes and couldn't help the short physical assessment she took of him. His hair reminded her of the wheat fields she'd seen as a child when she had accompanied her grandfather on his summer business trips through Ohio. And she wondered at the creased scar just beneath his left eye.

Yes, Jonah Deardon was a very handsome man. And he was now to be her husband. Emma had to work hard to remember her lessons to act a lady and not gawk at him.

It was hard to mistake the sound of the front door slamming open.

"Millie!" a male voice screamed out for the inn keeper with a hint of urgency from the same direction. It sounded like Jarvis.

Millie hustled from the kitchen, past the dining room. All three Deardon brothers and two other boarding house patrons filed out to see what was going on. Emma followed on their heels.

Jarvis stood in the open doorway holding two young ruffians by the scruff of their neck collars.

"Caught these two boys trying to break into that back room behind the kitchen through the window."

Both boys writhed against their captor, but Jarvis had a good firm grip on them.

"We didn't hurt nothing," one boy squealed.

Emma had no idea what the boys possibly could have been looking for in that room. There was nothing but food stuffs. Maybe they were hungry.

Millie must've had the same thought.

"You boys wantin' some fresh vittles? We're just sitting down to supper and there are a couple of empty chairs at my table."

"What are you doing, Millie" Jarvis looked stunned. His mouth hung open and his eyes were nearly as wide as saucers. "You don't reward criminals. They were going to steal from you and you're going to feed them?"

"We wasn't gonna steal from Miss Millie," the bigger of the two boys said indignantly. "That fella said we just needed to get him the travelling bag from that room with the broken handles and he'd pay us two whole dollars. Each."

"I don't keep my travelling bags in th—"

"*My* travelling bag has broken handles," Emma said quietly, almost to herself. But the reason anyone would want that old thing was anybody's guess. There was nothing in there but her clothes, a few mementos of her family, and the deed to the Oregon property—which no one else knew about.

All eyes fell on her.

"Why would anybody want my old bag?"

"How did they know the handle was broken?" Noah asked.

"And how did they know she was staying in that room?" Lucas took a step toward Jarvis.

Everyone turned to look at the boys, whom Jarvis still had by their necks.

They looked at each other and shrugged.

"Where is the man who offered you the money?" Jonah inquired.

"And what did he look like," Noah asked in succession.

After getting a brief description of the man and a location where they were supposed to meet him, Jarvis let go of the boys and they both scrambled to follow Millie to the kitchen with the deputy right behind them.

"You boys go check it out," he told the Deardons. "I'll stay and watch over the ladies." He glanced at Emma and tugged on the front of the hat he wore. "Oh," he said in afterthought to the men, "you may want to take the lantern there with you. It's getting pretty dark outside."

One by one, Jonah, Noah, and Lucas all grabbed their hats from the rack in the entrance and Lucas picked up the lantern that hung from an oversized nail next to the doorway before stepping out into the night.

"Stay put," Jonah warned Emma.

He stood so close to her that her neck had to crane backward to see his face. The look in his eyes said there was no room for argument and she took one step away from him.

Apparently satisfied, he disappeared into the darkening twilight.

The nerve.

"There's no one here," Lucas said throwing his hands through his hair.

Jonah scanned the street for anything suspicious. He was still fairly unfamiliar with St. Joseph and that irked him. If Emma was in some sort of danger, wasn't it now his job to protect her? He couldn't very well do that if he didn't know what he needed to protect her against.

"Let's get back to the boarding house," Jonah told his brothers. "We'll leave first thing in the morning for Stone Creek." Now that they'd delivered their herd and found Miss Foster, there was no reason for them to stay.

As they started down the street toward Millie's, the light in the lantern flickered out and Jonah stopped. A sudden feeling in his gut told him that someone was watching them. He squinted his eyes at the dark. The sun had all but disappeared behind the horizon and the moon was little more than a sliver. He couldn't see anything but shadows. If someone lurked in the obscurity, it would serve them best to return to Millie's as quickly as possible.

"Jonah, we should stay close together," Noah called from a few steps in front of him.

His brother was right.

When they got back to the boarding house, the two young boys who'd tried to break in were sitting on the top step of the stairs, each handcuffed to either side of the porch railing. Jonah and his brothers stepped into the house and found Emma, Millie, and Jarvis all sitting in the parlor with a small blaze glowing in the fireplace. They all stood up.

Jonah shook his head. "We couldn't find anyone out there." He turned to Millie. "But, all the same, I think it's best if we head on out at first light."

Emma stood, her hands clasped together in front of her.

Jonah stepped forward, his heart pounding heavily against his chest, which perturbed him greatly.

Control, Deardon.

"We'd like to get this marriage thing all sorted out, ma'am. But, I would feel more comfortable if we finished our—" he choked on the next word, "business…at Redbourne Ranch."

"Oh," she lifted a hand to her neck, her fingers caressing the deep indent there. "I thought it had already been decided. Aren't *you* taking your brother's place in the agreement, Mr. Deardon?"

Jonah shot a look at his brothers, who were both looking down at the food on their plates with keen interest.

Traitors.

He lifted an eyebrow and looked at Emma hard, but couldn't tell if she was teasing or if she simply just didn't care which of them she married. He pulled at the collar on his shirt. It was loose enough, so why did he feel like he could scarcely breathe?

He cleared his throat.

"That has been discussed," Jonah affirmed, stretching his neck to one side, then the other. He glanced at Millie, who eyed him with keen interest, then around to Jarvis and his brothers before returning his eyes to her. Noah and Lucas looked pleased as punch and Jonah had the sudden urge to knock the smiles right off their faces.

He cleared his throat again. "So, Millie, do you have any rooms left for tonight? I don't want Miss Foster sleeping in that room. I'll settle her account in the morning."

"Yes. Yes, of course. I'll just put some fresh linens on the bed and it'll be ready for Miss Emma in no time at all," Millie said, reaching for another lantern on the table next to the armed chair she'd been sitting in when they'd returned. "Oh, and Jarvis?" she said looking at the deputy. "Be a dear and let those boys go. They're not going to hurt anyone and I think they've learned their lesson.

Jarvis rolled his eyes, but reached for his keys as he swung the front door wide.

Emma headed toward the kitchen to collect her things.

"I'll fetch them and bring them up to you," Jonah said as he stepped in front of her, effectively blocking her path. "You go with Millie."

For a moment it looked as if she was going to argue with him, but she turned and stomped toward the staircase.

You're just making one good impression after another, Deardon.

"Wait," he called after her before she reached the stairs.

Emma turned around, hand on hips and a look that would quell a bear.

"Why is there a man following you? Who is he?"

She stared at him.

Silence.

Jonah could see the muscles in her face pulsating at her jawline. She was angry. He could see it in her eyes. They looked like the sea in the midst of a storm. Beautiful.

Emma did not grace him with an answer, but turned and trailed up the stairs without so much as a look back.

"Women," he grumbled.

When he walked into the pantry, Jonah realized he had no idea what things belonged to Emma. He glanced over the small makeshift bed made up in the corner of the room. A fairly large travelling case, tucked neatly under the cot, protruded slightly and a brown leather satchel sat on top of the folded patchwork blanket.

Jonah reached under the bed and pulled the corner of the travelling case until it was mostly exposed. He grabbed a hold of the handle and it gave way. A sigh of relief emerged from his throat when the latches on either side of the case remained closed and nothing came spilling out to his view. He pulled the case up under one of his arms and strung the satchel over his neck and shoulder.

He turned into a damp sort of flimsy cloth that draped over his face.

"What in the…"

He tried to brush it from his face, but every movement seemed to tangle him even further. When he finally was able to pry himself loose, he backed away from the fabric. The material had been hung from a string suspended across the width of the room and he sniggered at the irony of his little trap. A thin chemise top and set of bloomers, hanging to dry, had gotten the best of him.

"Getting a little ahead of yourself aren't you, big brother?" Noah leaned against the doorway with his arm above his head and a grin spread across his face.

"Funny."

The smile on his brother's face grew wider—if that were possible.

Jonah stepped forward in attempt to pass Noah and leave the walk-in pantry.

"You seem awfully protective of Miss Foster all of the sudden," his brother said before he could make it through the door. "If I didn't know any better, I would say you've taken a liking to your unwanted bride."

Jonah stopped mid stride. "I still don't like it. The idea of marrying some woman just for her dowry. I feel responsible for her is all. She's only here because of the agreement Dad and Henry made with her grandfather."

"Doesn't hurt that her eyes are the color of the glow around the moon at midnight either," Lucas interjected in their conversation as he joined Noah in blocking Jonah's retreat.

"You're quite the poet, Lucas." Jonah flexed his jaw. "This room is suddenly too small." Jonah pushed his way past them both and marched up the stairs.

It irked him that his brothers had noticed her eyes. Of course, why wouldn't they? Her eyes were mesmerizing and he was naïve if he believed for one moment that he was the only man to notice them.

Emma paced the new room she'd been assigned for the night. As if she wouldn't have told him or Millie or Jarvis, the deputy, if she'd known that someone was following her—if she'd thought for one moment that she was in danger. How dare Jonah Deardon treat her as if she were a senseless child?

Why would someone follow her or want her old worn out travelling case anyway? She had nothing of real value, and if it was lady companionship this man desired, there were plenty of brothels around—not that a real lady should know anything about them. Had it not been for the little gatherings her governess had thrown for some of her more brazen friends after their lessons, she'd haven't an idea.

Emma, of course, had never been invited, but she'd often crawled into her oversized closet and listened to their shameless talk and giggling through the paper thin walls. She'd learned more than at those events than she ever did in her geography lessons. Most of all, they taught her what she didn't want to be like.

Emma lay down on the bed, which she had to admit was a lot cozier than the small cot she'd had in the pantry. For some reason, she felt safe with the Deardons around. Somehow she knew that Jonah would not let anything happen to her. She turned onto her side and played with the strings that protruded from the quilt covering on the bed.

If she could be trained to be a lady, there was hope for Jonah Deardon yet. She lay back onto one of the large pillows that decorated the bed. If she had to be away from her beloved Orchard House in Boston, being Mrs. Devastatingly Handsome, didn't seem so bad.

What could go wrong?

CHAPTER SEVEN

"You've got to be joking." Jonah looked out his bedroom window to see a ray of sunlight dimmed by the storm clouds rolling in. He'd heard reports from other riders that Kansas was experiencing a tremendous drought and yet their trip to Stone Creek was going to be a wet one. He guessed he should be grateful that his cousins lived in eastern Kansas where apparently they were still getting rain.

"I'll be back in a half hour with the extra horse from the stables for Miss Foster," Jonah told Lucas, who was still trying to pull on his boots through the grogginess of sleep. "Make sure she's ready."

The short trip to the Pony Express stables, where they'd been looking after the mare selected for Emma to ride on the trail down to Stone Creek, took nearly twice as long as Jonah had expected. Despite the weather, he'd made pretty good time getting there, but it had taken him nearly a quarter hour to wake the sleeping stable-hand.

Jonah tied the mare next to his gelding in front of the stone entry steps to the yard. The horse was a beautiful brown and white paint with spots on her nose and from what he'd seen on the trail, she seemed to ride smoothly over the harsh terrain and had been even-tempered and alert.

Perfect for a lady, he thought.

He rubbed the mare's nose, then turned and made his way up to the house. He hoped that by this time, Millie would have something made up for breakfast. They needed to get on the road, and starting the day off with a warm cooked meal would make all the difference.

"Are you insane? You can't possibly…"

Jonah rounded the corner in time to see the horrified expression on Emma's face. The moment her eyes locked with his, she immediately darted around Lucas and marched right up to him.

"I have never been on a horse in my life. I've barely even laid eyes on them. How can you expect me to…to ride?"

She was standing too close to him.

He knew she was speaking, but Jonah couldn't concentrate on the words. He liked watching her lips move and had the sudden urge to reach out and crush her to him. To comfort her. To kiss her.

Where did that come from?

Focus, Deardon.

"Stone Creek is only a couple of day's ride from here. I'm sure you're a natural. Besides, we'll stop in one of the town's along the way to rest. You'll be fine," he managed to say.

"Only a couple of day's ri…" Emma threw her hands in the air and walked over to Millie.

Jonah groaned.

The back of her dress swung back and forth with the gentle sway of her full hips as she moved. He had to change the direction of his thoughts.

Now.

"Well, you certainly won't be able to ride in that dress." He cleared his throat.

Emma gasped as she shot a surprised look at him.

"And just what is wrong with my dress?" she asked, her hands on her hips.

"Nothing from where I'm standing, but trying to ride side saddle is going to get mighty uncomfortable after a half-minute or so." Jonah couldn't help the smirk that formed on his lips at her look of affront. "You'll want something with a split skirt. Or britches."

"Why, I never." Emma looked to Millie for help.

"We'll find something for you, dear," Millie said with an uneasy smile.

She linked her arm through Emma's and together they walked past the dining room to the stairs.

Noah walked up behind Jonah. "Maybe we should just buy a wagon."

"If she's going to be living out west, she'll need to know how to ride a horse. No wagon."

Noah clapped him on the shoulder. "For a lady, she sure is a handful."

Emma's things were no longer sitting next to the doorway. Jonah must have already taken them out to the horses to secure for travel.

Horses.

Her grandfather had arranged riding lessons for her a few years back, but she had insisted on learning to play the piano instead. Why hadn't she just listened and learned how to ride?

Truth be told, she was scared of the fascinating creatures. They towered over her and they were always surrounded by flies. And they smelled.

By the time Emma returned, Jonah and his brothers had already finished their breakfast. Lucas leaned back in his chair while the other two sat with their elbows on the table. She cleared her throat and they all looked up at her appraisingly.

She pouted her lips, then rolled them inward. A hand darted to the curls that spilled from her coiffure. The trousers were too big and were held up by a strip of cloth Millie cut from an old piece of fabric, and the shirt she wore looked like it could fit any of the Deardon brothers. She was sure she looked a sight.

Millie had held onto a few things guests at the boarding house had left behind over the years. Luckily, there had been a few pieces of men's clothing in the lot.

"Happy now?" she asked with an air of defiance.

"Why yes, yes I am," Jonah said, standing in place at the table.

Heat rose instantly in her cheeks. Her eyes locked with his and the warmth spread all the way down to her toes. She was pleased at his reaction. Somehow, it mattered what Jonah Deardon thought.

Noah and Lucas scrambled to their feet.

"Just need a hat and the ensemble will be complete."

Millie stepped into the dining room at that precise moment and plopped an old, droopy hat on top of her head and continued on into the kitchen.

Noah's face was the first to crack into a smile. Then, they all burst out into laughter. Including Emma. She reached up and tugged the hat from her head.

Lucas pulled out a chair and placed a slice of Millie's bread on a plate in front of her. Noah slid the jar of preserves across the table, and Jonah poured her a glass of freshly steamed apple cider before clearing their plates and taking them into the kitchen.

The bread was still warm and Millie's blackberry preserves were wonderful. However, Emma didn't have long to enjoy her meal.

"The trail is going to be a muddy mess by now," Jonah

said as he pulled out Emma's chair…with her still in it. "We need to go."

Emma shoved the last bite of her bread into her mouth and stood up.

That's not what a lady would do, her grandfather's words echoed in her mind from the many times he'd told her before.

The rain outside was steady, but not as heavy as she had expected. She put on the hat Millie had given her and pulled it down over her ears. A little water never hurt anyone. Right?

When she reached the top step of the stone staircase leading out of the yard, she froze. The horses were even larger than she remembered. She had no idea how she would be able to stay atop such a beast.

Millie hugged each of the boys, then followed Jonah's gaze up to Emma. The kind caretaker pranced up the three steps and pulled her into a quick embrace.

"Be careful," she cautioned. Then, she pulled away, still clutching at Emma's arms, the rain dripping down her uncovered head. "I hope everything turns out the way you want it to."

Emma nodded. "Thank you for everything, Millie."

The woman patted Emma's arms briefly at the shoulder, picked up the hems of her dress, and darted for the house.

Emma's focus again returned to the horses. Noah and Lucas were already mounted. Jonah had the reins for the brown and white pony in his hand and motioned for her to join him. She didn't move.

"Don't make me carry you, woman," he said firmly, not taking his eyes off hers.

She looked down at the first step in front of her and then back to the horse.

Stop being such a ninny, she thought. *You can do this. You can do hard things.*

With one long breath she moved her feet and covered the

distance between them in moments.

Jonah nodded his approval.

Emma looked from him to the horse.

"Penny, meet Miss Foster." Jonah reached down and took Emma's hand in his and guided it up to the horse's broad nose.

Emma had been expecting the hair to be more like the fur of a fluffy puppy, and was surprised by the soft short bristles of her wet face. She glanced up to Jonah, who smiled reassuringly.

"Penny? She's a girl then?"

When Jonah confirmed, Emma felt a little better.

"Now that you two have been acquainted, can we get on the road?"

Without warning, Jonah lifted her from the ground and swung Emma's legs over the saddle. It was slick from the rain and Emma's bottom slid around a little before she felt settled into the seat.

"Here are your reins. Pull left to go left." He motioned left with his hands holding imaginary straps. "Pull on the right to go right. Hold them steady to go straight, and pull both back at the same time to stop."

He thought he could give her a few short sentences and she would magically know how to ride? She stared at him blankly.

"There's nothing to be afraid of," Jonah said as he climbed his own mount. "I'll be right here."

Noah and Lucas started out first and Jonah followed. Emma lifted the reins, but the horse didn't move.

"Come on, Penny girl. Go," she urged.

Nothing.

"Come on, girl," Emma said as she bounced a little in the saddle.

Still nothing.

What had Jonah told her to do? She tried pulling the reins to the right and wonderfully Penny understood her instructions and turned to the right. Emma kept pulling until she finally faced the same direction as the others.

"Give her a little nudge with your heels," Jonah encouraged, obviously finding enjoyment in her discomfort.

It worked. However, Emma had been unprepared for the initial bump in movement and fell forward—the saddle handle jabbing her in the ribs. It only took a moment before Jonah had pulled up alongside her.

"Are you all right?" he inquired.

Emma sat up straight. "If this knob contraption hadn't been in the way, I would be much better."

Jonah laughed. "It's called a horn."

"I don't care what it's called. It hurts." Emma grimaced at the ache in her side. This was going to be a long ride.

CHAPTER EIGHT

Jonah looked up at the menacing clouds looming overhead. There had been a light drizzle most of the day. It seemed as if the storm in St. Joseph had followed them. If the growing darkness was any indication, it was only a matter of time before the sky broke and the trail would become dangerous.

As if the gathering storm wasn't enough to worry about, several times over the last hour Jonah had glanced behind them to see if anyone followed. There had been no one in sight, but it was growing increasingly harder to see as their terrain grew more clustered with high rolling hills and deep valleys.

Jonah glanced over at Emma. He'd stayed slightly behind her all morning to help provide a sense of security, but as the rain grew heavier, she sat back farther on the saddle, hunched down closer to the saddle horn, and hugged it in to her.

She was frightened, yet even after travelling near most the day in the rain with only a few stops along the way, he had not heard one complaint. She just clung to the reins of that horse as if they were her lifeline.

A bolt of lightning split the sky immediately followed by a roaring boom of thunder. In seconds, torrents of rain dumped on top of them. Emma's horse, Penny, danced about at the sudden friction in the air. All of the horses had become a little uneasy.

Noah turned his mount around and pulled up next to Jonah.

"There's a small town just over the next hill. I think we can make it that far in a good twenty minutes," Noah was practically screaming the words to be heard above the storm. "We can find a place there to hole up for the night."

Emma looked up at Noah, then back at Jonah. Her hair had fallen into her face with rivulets of water running down her cheeks. She shivered. She had a chill, but it wouldn't do him any good to give her a blanket now, it would just be soaked within moments.

Jonah nodded to Noah. "Let's go."

Penny's head lifted in the air and turned toward the east with her ears rigid and pointing forward. The mare sensed something that Jonah couldn't see and before he could reach out and grab ahold of her reins, another loud crack of thunder rumbled through the heavens. The horse bolted forward with an unsuspecting Emma clinging tightly to the reins and gripping the edges of the saddle.

She didn't scream.

Jonah whistled and slapped the reins of his horse.

"Hi-yah!" he yelled and Perseus quickly burst out after the mare. Jonah's heart nearly jumped from his chest as visions of Henry being thrown from the mustang flooded his memory.

Rain slashed at his face. He kept his head low, grateful for the brim of his hat that protected his eyes and allowed him to see and follow the direction of the spooked horse.

Another flash of Henry's strong body slamming against the rock hard ground pushed its way into his mind. His brother had been an experienced horseman, but Miss Foster was a novice. She had no idea how to handle a horse. He flicked the reins again, urging his mount even faster.

Moments felt an eternity, but finally he caught up to her. The reins dragged on the ground. Emma's knuckles were white from gripping the saddle on either side of the horn. Jonah pulled up alongside Penny, attempting to keep time with the galloping horse, and reached out for the bridle.

His fingers grazed the leather, but the rain had made it too slippery to hold onto. He looked at the woman gripping the saddle for dear life.

"Emma," he called loudly, but the sound was lost in the wind. If he could just get her to look at him, maybe he could pull her onto his own horse. "Emma!" he screamed even louder.

She shifted her head enough to look at him. He held out his hand, but she shook her head and returned her gaze to the back of the spooked mare's neck. Jonah rode as close as he dared and once again extended his hand out to her, palm up. Emma glanced at his hand and he motioned for her to take it with a flick of his fingers.

She met his eyes and for a brief moment he saw her attempt to muster the courage to try. She let go of her grip on the saddle with one hand and started to draw her hand toward his, but when the horse bucked a little, she quickly retracted it.

Damn.

Emma's back rose and fell with deep breaths as if trying to calm herself. She finally reached out again and this time Jonah was able to gain a firm grip on her forearm. He pulled and she flew off the wild paint and onto his horse and he tucked her into the folds of his arms and slowed the gelding to a stop.

"Emma, look at me," Jonah said taking her head into both hands.

She shook her head.

"Come on, look at me."

"No," she said firmly, a quiver in her voice.

"Why not?" He brushed a sopping lock from her forehead and tucked it behind her ear.

"Because I don't want you to see me cry." She hiccupped and laughed at the same time.

Jonah placed a finger below her chin and lifted her face upward, exposing her face to the weather. Her eyes flitted a moment to his, then closed, releasing a plump tear through her lashes and down her cheek with an assembly of raindrops.

When Emma opened her eyes again, they were still wet and the light from the small moon peeking through the storm clouds now caused them to glimmer.

Jonah stared at her, amazed. She was the most incredible woman. Strong. And beautiful.

His hands delved into the hair behind her ears, his thumb lazily brushing the rain and tears away. Slowly, he bent his head toward hers, but was stopped abruptly by the rim of his hat colliding with hers. He laughed.

She bit her lip. A slight giggle escaped.

Emma reached up and pulled the hat from her head and leaned into Jonah's body, allowing the rain to fall unencumbered down her face.

"You did good," he said against her ear.

She *felt* good against him and he tightened his grip around her and with another short chuckle doubled back toward his brothers.

Jonah didn't love the idea of leaving the mare out here in the storm, but right now he had to make sure Emma was safe.

"Penny?" Lucas asked when they'd rejoined him and Noah at the top of the hill.

"Still running," was all Jonah said in response with a flick of his head.

They understood and both Noah and Lucas rode after the mare.

What had spooked the horse Jonah was still unsure, but he was grateful everyone was safe. He was tired and admittedly a little sore and couldn't imagine the stiffness Miss Foster was going to feel in the morning. He urged Perseus to a light canter. He needed her out of his lap for now or his thoughts would be relentless and hard to control for the rest of the trip.

Stone Creek, Kansas

Emma had believed St. Joseph to be a small town compared to her beloved Boston, but Stone Creek and Redbourne Ranch were in the middle of nowhere. All she could see in any direction were hills and farms followed by hills and more farms.

Although the rain had let up since last night, Jonah had insisted that she ride with him the rest of the way. He'd been very sweet with her last night, making sure she had something warm to sleep in and food in her belly. Then, he'd propped himself up in a chair outside of her door at the town's small inn, and slept.

For the first time since her grandfather's passing, she'd felt…safe.

This morning, he'd set her in the saddle and had climbed up behind her. She had to admit that she liked the feel of his arms around her and his chest against her back. Familiar alarms of propriety screamed at her, but what other choice did she have?

Emma opened her mouth to ask Jonah for a drink of water, but closed it again when he held out the open large metal flask. She turned and looked up at him. A lady did not drink spirits.

"It's a canteen," Jonah said. He must have sensed her hesitation. "With water in it."

"Thank you." Gratefully, she took the container into her hands and allowed the liquid to pass through her lips. When some of the water dripped down her chin, she pulled away and wiped the excess with her thumb.

"Thirsty?" Jonah asked with a little chuckle.

It had been nearly an hour since Emma had seen the last little farmhouse and she wondered just how much farther it would be to this Redbourne Ranch. They'd sat in silence most of the way. She had so many questions, but guessed they would be better asked once they'd gotten settled.

Emma was still unsure of why they were headed to Stone Creek instead of getting on their way to Oregon. One thing was for sure though—she was not going to make the trek across the country sharing a horse with Jonah.

When they peaked a particularly large hill, a massive home with several outbuildings, including a large barn, stables, and an enormous corral came into view. Horses and other livestock roamed the fields inside thick wooden fences.

"We're here," Noah yelled from just ahead.

The excitement that sparked the air was nearly tangible and with a quick flick of the reins, Jonah's horse, Perseus, launched forward. Emma gasped, but relaxed as Jonah's arms tightened around her and his soft laugh sounded in her ear.

"They're here," a young boy yelled, running alongside them as they rode into the yard. He used a stick to keep his large metal hoop spinning.

More children ran from the house as they approached the front porch steps and several ranch hands joined them.

Jonah dismounted as did Noah and Lucas. A beautiful woman with hair near the same color as Jonah's ran down the stairs to greet them. She grinned and pulled them all into a fierce embrace.

Emma watched with curiosity from atop Jonah's horse. She'd never really been around large families and wasn't sure what to expect or what would be expected of her.

When the woman released Jonah and his brothers, she glanced up at Emma.

"And this must be Miss Foster." She stepped around Lucas, who'd picked up a little girl, spinning her about.

Jonah quickly stepped in front of the woman and held up a hand for Emma. She placed her hands on his shoulders and slid down easily.

"Hello." She wasn't sure what else to say. "I'm Emma."

"Why aren't you the prettiest thing? And would you look at those eyes, Jonah? Henry's a lucky man."

Jonah's face fell. Lucas set the little girl back on the ground and both he and Noah stepped up to join their little group.

"Where *is* Henry?" When the woman looked at Jonah's face, her smile dropped. "Jonah," she said his name slowly, "where is Henry?"

"Aunt Leah," Jonah began.

Noah stepped up behind her and put his arm around her shoulders.

"It was an accident," Lucas said. "A mustang threw him."

Emma's heart swelled painfully as Leah's face contorted in anguish and tears started down her face. She hunched over, her arms folded across her stomach, and Noah eased her down as she dropped to the ground on her bottom.

"Jonah, Noah, Lucas," she looked at each of them with tear-filled eyes, "I am so sorry," she said in a barely audible voice.

"Mama?" A young voice pulled Emma's attention to the little boy who'd been spinning the metal ring when they'd arrived. He stood with his stick still in hand, his eyebrows crumpled in the middle with concern.

Leah reached out and put an arm around him and he rested his head in the crook of her neck and she kissed him on the top of his head.

"Why are you crying, Mama?"

She didn't respond. It seemed she couldn't.

The other children quickly joined him at their mother's skirt. The little girl crawled up onto Leah's lap and leaned back against her other arm. Jonah, Noah, and Lucas also sat down, each now with their arm around one of the remaining three older boys.

Emma felt like an intruder on such a tender moment. She hadn't known Henry. Henry Deardon had been a name she'd learned at just fifteen years old when her grandfather had arranged their betrothal. She wasn't a part of this and wanted to leave the family to their grief.

Around the side of the house it looked as if there may be a garden where she could go and wait a while. Emma took a step backward, but Jonah reached out and caught her hand in his.

"Stay," he whispered, pulling her gently toward him on the ground.

She sat down and immediately the little girl scooted from her mother's lap and climbed onto hers.

Leah reached a hand out to her and Emma quickly placed her own inside it. "The wedding," she said softly. She must have believed that Henry's death had been a devastating loss for Emma. Emma thought she might cry herself from the look of pain and sympathy on Leah's face.

"Are you Miss Foster?" the little girl asked with surprising clarity for a child.

"Mmhmm," Emma answered positively. "How did you know?"

"'Cause Mama said it would take an angel to marry Hank, and you're the prettiest angel I've ever seen."

Emma looked around at all of the faces now staring at her.

It took a moment, but Leah was the first to laugh. Then Jonah. The rest followed.

Leah wiped the tears from her eyes and face and stood up, keeping her young son's hand curled in her own. "Come on, that's enough fretting for now. I'm sure our guests would like to get settled in, don't you think, Cole?" She mustered a smile, but her eyes were still wet and red.

The boy nodded his head excitedly.

Jonah pulled Emma to her feet, but did not immediately let go of her hand. She wasn't sure if it was simply to help her feel more at ease or if it had something to do with the wonderful kiss they'd nearly shared last night.

I wasn't imagining it. He was going to kiss me. Right?

Emma looked down when she felt a little tug on her skirt. The little girl smiled up at her, then slid her small hand into Emma's. "I bet you'll be the most beautiful bride."

Heat rose in Emma's cheeks and she glanced over at Jonah.

"I think so," he said matter-of-factly.

She knew she should be shocked by how forward Jonah was with her, but she liked knowing he thought she was pretty. She bit her bottom lip, then glanced down at the child.

"What's your name sweetheart? How old are you?" Emma asked, leaning down closer to the girl.

"Hannah. And I'm six." She smiled, revealing two missing teeth.

"Well, Hannah, I think you'll make a beautiful bride one day too." Emma squeezed her hand.

Hannah's smile widened until it touched her eyes.

Emma stood up and caught Jonah's stare.

"Six?" she mouthed at him.

Jonah winked.

Emma smiled to herself. Little Hannah was quite grown up for six.

A beautiful bride? Emma didn't dare hope—wasn't sure she wanted to.

"Shall we?" Jonah asked, sweeping the air in front of him.

The two girls giggled and walked past him, up the front porch stairs, and into the main house.

This was going to be an adventure. Emma just hoped she was ready.

CHAPTER NINE

Mornings at Redbourne Ranch were as beautiful as he'd remembered. He'd spent a few weeks here just after his mother'd left and had been back a few times over the years when the work would allow.

The misty haze that rose off the pond combined with a glint of the sun reflecting off the water added an almost magical feel to the place. Jonah sat on the swing Uncle Jameson had built for his children off a low-hanging branch of an old maple tree to think.

He gazed out across the field behind the pond where the grass had been cut low to the ground and a gaggle of chairs had been orchestrated in two rows facing a feeding loft that had been swept clean. Large bows made of thin material graced wooden posts that had been set strategically around the designated area. Henry would have liked the set up.

So much had changed in the last month, and now, his whole life was about to change again. Duty told him he needed to take responsibility for their family's commitment to Mr. Foster and marry Emma for her dowry, but reason told him to simply pay Emma handsomely for the Oregon land and walk away from further obligation. Neither option sat well with him.

When he saw Raine, Leah's oldest son open the doors to the first stable, Jonah jumped off the swing and followed him. When they'd arrived last night, Uncle Jameson and the three oldest Redbourne boys had been over to the neighbors delivering some fresh vegetables and helping rebuild a wind damaged barn. When they'd returned, Jonah and his brothers had scarcely a moment to speak with them before bedtime.

"Morning, Jonah," Raine greeted him.

"Raine."

"That swing sure does help when you have something on your mind to work out."

"You often have a lot to work out, do you?" Jonah teased.

Raine smiled as he grabbed a brush hanging from a nail just outside one of the stall gates.

"Raine," one of the twins whispered as he poked his head around the door. "Have you seen Genesis? He's gotten away again and I'm afraid mama will find him before we do."

Levi and Taggert were nearly identical, barring the long, thin scar on Tag's neck where a bobcat cub had gotten him.

"Jonah?" The twin stood up straight and walked into the stable. It was Levi. No scar. "Are Noah and Lucas up?"

"I haven't seen them yet this morning, but I'm sure if you go get them, they would be happy to help you find your creature."

Levi spun on his heel, but before he rounded the corner he turned back. "Sorry about Henry, Jonah. That's rough."

Jonah nodded his appreciation.

"So, what's on your mind this morning that got you up earlier than the rest of us with chores to do?" Raine asked, still brushing the pony.

Jonah recounted Emma's experience with Penny.

"Use Allouette here," Raine told him, now holding up a bucket of oats to the beautiful white mare with a dark brown mane. "We call her Lou for short. We got her when Hannah was first learning how to ride. She's real gentle." He set the bucket down and retrieved one of the dull red apples from the basket on top of the work table at the far edge of the stable.

"Does she spook?" The last thing Jonah needed was to have another horse go rogue with Emma in tow.

"Not that I've ever seen," Raine answered. After rubbing the apple on the bottom of his shirt, he placed it in his open palm and fed it to Lou. "So, what are you going to do?"

"I'm sorry?"

"About Miss Foster." Raine threw Jonah a shovel. "You obviously like her."

"What does a sixteen-year-old scalawag like you know about it?" Jonah was irked that he could be read so easily—especially by his young cousin.

Raine chuckled. "Enough."

Jonah spent the rest of the early morning helping Raine and the others finish their chores. Aunt Leah had assured him that she would take good care of Emma and not to worry. He determined that he would wait to teach her how to ride until after lunch.

It was nice to be around family.

After the plank on the corral fence had been mended, Jonah pulled the bucket up out of the well. It had very little water, but he was able to manage half a cup of cool liquid. He leaned back against the stones and took a deep breath.

"Jonah," Leah opened the back door and walked down the back steps from the house, "may I have a word?"

Jonah wiped the small droplets of excess water from his mouth with the back of his hand and set the tin cup on the ledge of the well.

Uncle Jameson, with two large beams balanced on his shoulder, intercepted her on his way to the barn. He set the poles on the ground, grabbed her about the waist, and kissed her smack dab on the mouth for God and everyone to see. After a moment, he pulled away without a single word, recovered his load, and walked away, whistling.

Jonah just stared—as did half the people in the yard.

Aunt Leah smiled as if the display had been the most normal thing in the world, although she looked a little flushed when she reached him. She jumped up and sat on the well wall with one leg curled under her, turned enough so she could face him.

"Jonah, dear, the wedding was supposed to be the day after tomorrow. I had thought with Henry being gone and all—"

"Dad asked me to take Henry's place," Jonah said before she could finish.

"I see."

"I told him I didn't want to pay for Henry's mistakes, but then..."

"But then you met Emma."

Jonah nodded.

"She is a lovely girl, Jonah. Right smart. And I would venture she's mighty capable and a quick learner," Leah said with a smirk. "She's in the kitchen with Lottie right now, learning how to knead bread. I think she's taking out all of her recent frustrations on the dough." She laughed. Then her face became serious. "You don't have to marry her, you know."

Jonah snorted. "Tell that to my father."

"I love my brother, but Gabe is too stubborn for his own good." Leah put her hand on Jonah's shoulder. "He's let his pride and fear get in the way of what's most important. You and your brothers. His family. Us. Don't let that happen to you."

He thought for a moment. "I saw what mama's leaving

did to my dad and I vowed that I would never let a woman have that kind of power over me. I thought I would be perfectly happy never getting married."

"What?" Aunt Leah jumped down off of the well wall and turned to face him with her hands on her hips. "Jonah Nicholas Deardon, why on earth would you say such a thing? You'll make a fine husband and father. Why would you ever choose not to have such a blessing in your life?"

Jonah was taken aback by her sudden effrontery.

"Aunt Leah," he said quietly, "I've changed my mind."

Leah had opened her mouth as if ready with a response, but she quickly closed it again.

"I want what you and Uncle Jameson have. I want a big family with a ranch of my own. I'm just not sure I want it all right now."

"Jonah," Noah called, running toward the stables, "mount up. Uncle Jameson needs our help."

Jonah leaned over and kissed his aunt on her cheek. "Thank you."

He rushed after his brother and found Lucas and Uncle Jameson, along with three of his young cousins, mounted and ready to ride just outside the stable doors.

"A small herd of buffalo have tromped onto Redbourne land and some of the surrounding farms, destroying many of the farmers' crops," Jameson told them. "Rafe," he pointed at the youngest of them, "are you sure you want to ride along. It's going to be dangerous."

"Yes, sir," the young man responded without hesitation. "I'm ready."

Jameson nodded, pride exuding from his face.

Rafe was twelve years old and as ready to ride as any of them. Jonah shook his head. He'd been here at the beginning of the summer and he'd swear that the youngster had grown half a foot in that time. He stepped into the stable where

Perseus had been lodged and led the chestnut gelding out of the gate into the yard, and mounted.

"Where are the twins?" Jameson asked his boys.

All of the young Redbournes averted their father's gaze. Jonah was sure the twins were causing havoc somewhere and didn't envy them when their father found out.

"Who knows what monstrosity those boys will discover next," Jameson said with exasperation. He put two fingers to his lips and let out a two-toned whistle.

A loud woman's scream came from the house and the two boys fled down the back stairs giggling. They ran to the stables and within seconds emerged with their mounts.

Jameson raised a single eyebrow at them. The smiles on their faces quickly turned solemn and they bowed their heads.

"Keep your eyes open for the mustangs," Jameson cautioned as he looked hard at each of the riders on this little venture. "They've been more excitable than usual as of late and I'm afraid the old stallion may make things a little difficult for us."

Jameson's horse danced anxiously.

"It will be best if we can wrangle the buffalo into the south pasture and mend the fence between our land and the Miller farm. I want to avoid a stampede at all costs."

Jameson pulled the head of his horse around and swung his hand in the air in a circular motion.

"Move out."

CHAPTER TEN

Emma draped across one of the wooden chairs at the kitchen table. She'd had no idea how much work went into making something as simple as bread. She had to admit that punching the dough had made her feel lighter somehow, as if all of her worries had melted away along with her strength. However, it did feel good to have made something with her own hands.

Lottie, the plump Spanish cook, had been more than patient with her. Emma looked down at her clothing. Luckily, Leah had provided her a thick apron to put over her blue dress or, she feared, the garment would have been a powdery, sticky mess by now.

From the corner of her eye, Emma caught movement on the table. She turned her head and looked down with a startled gasp. A blue-green lizard with two black rings around its neck scurried toward her.

She heard a low snigger come from the kitchen doorway and spotted the twins she'd met late last night peering around the wall. She guessed they had placed their friend on the table with hopes to spook her.

It wouldn't work.

She'd recently had a few days on a train with a few orphans who'd liked to play practical jokes, but this Emma was not the same woman she was a week ago.

The boys didn't know she'd seen them.

The animal stopped and bobbed its brown head as if looking where it could go next.

"Well, what are you, little one?" Emma asked, holding her hand out to the small creature.

She giggled when it climbed onto her palm and up her arm to her shoulder.

"Awwwwhh." The twins both cried with a tone of disappointment and Emma smiled inside.

A loud, very distinct two-toned whistle sounded from the yard.

The two young boys immediately emerged from the shadows in the doorway to the kitchen.

"Come on, Genesis." One of the twins picked up the lizard, looking slightly dejected.

Lottie walked back into the kitchen just in time to see the animal before the boy had successfully tucked it into his pocket. She screamed and grabbed ahold of the broom next to the counter. With one swing of the straw strapped end, she caught the twin who'd hidden Genesis in his pocket on his rear end.

"¡Ay de mí!" Lottie exclaimed as she fell down onto the chair next to Emma. "Those boys and their little animales will be the death of me."

Emma stood up and walked over to the window. She pulled back the curtain and peered out at the mounted group that looked ready to ride.

The back door opened and Leah walked in.

"Where are they going?" Emma asked, attempting to keep the apprehension from her voice.

"Cal, the foreman, spotted some buffalo heading this

direction and they are just going to ride out and head them off."

"Is that safe?"

"With Jonah and his brothers along everything should be fine." Leah wrapped her arm around Emma's shoulder and giggled. "It looks like you are wearing some of that bread."

Emma laughed, sure she looked a sight.

"Come on, we'll get it cleaned out of your hair and maybe later we can all go for a swim."

Emma felt her eyes grow wide. She couldn't swim.

"I...don't know how to swim exactly."

"Don't worry, honey. You'll learn."

"Again," Jonah said. Emma had both successfully mounted and dismounted four times.

Raine's suggestion of using Allouette, the white mare, had been inspired. The horse was perfect for Emma.

She climbed up onto the horse again, but instead of getting down, she took the reins in her hands and gently urged the mare forward with her heels. When she reached the edge of the yard, she didn't stop, but continued walking the horse forward.

"If I didn't know any better," Jonah yelled out to her, "I'd say you were trying to get away from me."

Emma looked back over her shoulder and smiled. She still looked a little unsure with her current circumstance, but she pulled her reins to the right and the horse obeyed the easy command. She beamed.

"You can stop now," he said.

She didn't.

Emma slowly maneuvered the reins to one hand and reached down to rub the mare on the neck, then transferred the straps back into both hands.

"All right, Miss Foster, you've had your fun," he called more loudly than before.

She was getting too far away for comfort. "Seriously, Emma!"

The horse and inexperienced rider disappeared from view behind the house. Jonah ran up on the other side of the yard, but short of crossing through the little creek that poured into the pond, he could not reach her.

Luckily, he'd kept Perseus saddled to ride alongside her later in the lesson to help her feel more comfortable. Apparently, she didn't need it. He mounted his horse and quickly cantered around the house and over the wooden bridge until he caught up to her.

Emma pulled tight on the reins and Allouette stopped.

"Leah went to all this trouble," she motioned with her chin to the area in the field that had been decorated for the wedding, "for me?"

And Henry.

"Let's head back. I still need to teach you how to brush her down and put away the tack."

It took a while, but she was finally able to turn the horse all the way around.

When they reached the stables, Jonah jumped down and tied Perseus to the hitching post. "I'll be right back for you, boy," he said with a good rub to the side of his neck.

The horse nickered in appreciation.

Emma swung her leg around like he'd taught her to do and lowered herself to the ground. He was glad he was standing behind her because when she turned to face him, she fell against his chest.

"I'm sorry. I guess my legs are just a little wobbly with all the riding we've done over the past couple of days." She gently pushed herself away. "Is my body supposed to hurt like this?" she asked innocently.

Jonah laughed more loudly than he'd intended. "She admits it at last."

She looked at him, apparently still expecting an answer.

"Yes, you should be very sore."

"Oh, good. Because I hurt…everywhere."

She smiled up at him and he thought the world was going to stop for one brief moment.

How did she keep doing that?

"Come on in, Miss Foster," one of the twins called from the middle of the pond. "The water is wonderful and it's not that deep. See? I'm standing."

Leah had lent Emma a bathing costume that looked an awful lot like one of her belted dresses on top and a pair of men's trousers on the bottom—except for the frills gathered on her legs between her knees and ankles with a bow. And she'd helped her pull her hair back away from her face with a ribbon.

"Are you Levi or Taggert?" Emma walked to the edge of the pond and dipped her bare toes inside the cool water.

They'd told her how hot it had been all summer long here in Kansas and how lucky they'd been to avoid a lot of the drought conditions that were prevalent throughout the western more part of the territory. Living close to two big rivers definitely had its advantages.

"I'm Tag," he responded.

She looked at him. Even though they were just fifteen years old, the twins still measured a good foot taller than she, so she figured if she just waded half way out to where Tag stood, she shouldn't get anything wet past her knees.

She could do that.

Male laughter reached her ears and she looked up to see Jonah, Noah, Lucas, and Raine, their sixteen-year-old cousin, walk out of the bunkhouse and toward the pond barefoot and wearing nothing but frayed denim trousers.

Emma's mouth went dry. Jonah's slender abdomen was chiseled into six smaller compartments. She'd never seen a man without his clothes on before. He was beautiful.

Casually, she placed one foot after the other, getting a little deeper in the water. She could not take her eyes off of Jonah. She liked watching him move and was amazed that he wasn't as sore as she felt. Another step forward and the floor disappeared from beneath her. She sunk. Water engulfed her.

Her arms reached out for something, someone to help her. Panic gripped her chest. She had no idea what to do. She'd never been swimming before. Her eyes snapped open under the murky water and she looked around. To her surprise, she glimpsed Levi standing on the pond floor with a smile on his face, then he seemed to just jump and he flew up toward the top.

She had to try. She pushed off the bottom with her feet. It seemed like it was working until her head connected with something very hard. Everything went dark.

CHAPTER ELEVEN

"How were we to know she couldn't swim?"

Emma opened one eye and then the other. An umbrella of people looked down at her. Jonah's was the first face that came into focus and she attempted to sit up. Her head hurt, so she lay back down and closed her eyes.

"Well, that was about as fun as I'd expected," she said with a snort.

Everyone laughed.

"Aw, she'll be all right," Noah's voice assured the rest.

Emma opened her eyes again. The small crowd had dissipated and she could feel the warmth of the fading sun on her face. She tried to sit up again. Jonah placed his hand on her back and helped her upright.

"Don't do that again," he whispered, leaning forward until his forehead touched hers.

"What happened…exactly?" she asked.

He pulled away to look her in the eyes. A smirk formulated on his lips.

"The twins. And me."

She furrowed her brows, not understanding the meaning of his words. "I saw Levi under the water."

"Yes. And Tag was standing on his shoulders to make you think the pond wasn't as deep as it was where they were."

She should have known. She liked the twins. They were fun and full of life. She would just have to be more aware next time, so they wouldn't get the best of her.

"And me. You didn't come up and Leah told me you couldn't swim, so I jumped in after you. I hadn't expected you to be on your way up and your…" he smiled at her sheepishly, then looked down at the ground, "your head connected with my elbow."

Emma laughed. "Of course it did. It is dangerous being around you, cowboy." She pushed at his chest and her fingers caught fire. His bare skin was warm to the touch and firm.

Jonah looked down at her hand and took it into his.

"Miss Foster. Emma, I—"

The clinkety-clank of the dinner bell sounded as Lottie called everyone in for supper.

Jonah stood up and threw a bath sheet around Emma's shoulders. He reached down, took her by the hands, and lifted her to her feet. She wasn't at all sure the chill that swept through her was from being wet. And when Jonah briskly rubbed her arms through the towel, her legs became a little like Millie's preserves.

"I don't know how you ladies think you can swim in a getup like that. There's just too much material to be able to do much of anything." Jonah dropped one of her hands, but kept the other tucked neatly in his own.

Emma couldn't help the disappointment that settled in her gut when he didn't finish what he was going to say. She knew that he had reservations about taking Henry's place and wondered if she was being unreasonable in her expectations. Maybe she should just try to sell them the part of her dowry the Deardons wanted, the Oregon property.

"Let's get you dried off and changed for supper. I mean…"

He cleared his throat. Was he actually blushing? It had to just be the brilliant pink hues of the new sunset reflecting off his face.

"I'll walk you into the house and you can retire to your

room to dry off and change for supper."

Lord help her, she was falling for Jonah Deardon. She looked down at their intertwined hands. He'd stepped in front of her to open the door and her gaze trailed his strong arm up his shoulder to his corded neck. Jonah was handsome and kind, though a little rough around the edges, but she liked that about him and she realized she didn't want him to marry her simply because she possessed the land he needed. She wanted more.

They stepped up into the kitchen. Jonah let go of her hand and Emma stepped toward the hall.

"I have something for you," Leah said, catching up with her and linking her arm with Emma's. Emma didn't miss the sparkle in Leah's eyes.

"What are you up to?"

Jonah threw a clean white button down shirt over his shoulders and grabbed his boots. The wedding was scheduled for tomorrow and they hadn't even talked about it. He had no idea what was going on in that pretty little head of hers and he still hadn't decided what he was prepared to do. Emma Foster certainly was the most beautiful woman he'd ever seen, but he hardly knew the woman. Did it matter?

He scrubbed his stubbled chin with the backs of his fingers. It was time for a shave, but it would have to wait. He walked out of the bunkhouse and sat down on the steps, shirt still undone, and pulled on his boots.

The kitchen was filled with the delicious aroma of a pot roast that had been cooking most of the day and Jonah's mouth started to water. He hadn't had a lot to eat for lunch and his stomach now reminded him rather loudly just how hungry he was. He sat down at the table where Lucas, Noah, and most of the children had already been seated.

He glanced up to see Emma standing next to Lottie near the stove. His heart lurched forward and he had to focus on keeping his breathing slow and steady.

She caught his stare, but didn't look away. She smiled. Her wet hair had been brushed and braided down one side of her face and was accented by branches of tiny white flowers.

Uncle Jameson opened the back door and walked inside. The twins followed, heads bowed. They walked up to Emma and muttered something Jonah couldn't hear, then quietly took their places at the table, but Jonah didn't miss the smirk that passed between them.

Emma joined them with two loaves of bread cradled in a kitchen cloth in her arms.

"Miss Foster made her first bread today," Leah said with a smile and a wink at Emma.

After Jameson took the loaves from her arms and set them on the bread board to cut, Emma found her seat next to Jonah and sat down, a satisfied grin on her face.

"Congratulations," he whispered next to her ear.

"Thank you," she said with a brief glance in his direction. Her yellow dress added depth to her eyes.

They enjoyed the meal and were just finishing up when there was a knock on the front door.

"Excuse me," Aunt Leah said as she stood and left the room.

A few moments later, she returned with a young girl with ringlets and ribbons in her hair. Raine pushed his seat backward and stood, wiping the corners of his mouth with his napkin.

The twins giggled, but their delight was cut short with one look from their father.

"Sarah," Raine said in a slightly cracked voice, "what are you doing here."

"Jameson," Leah looked at her husband, "the Millers wanted to say thank you for driving those buffalo off their farm and they've sent a bottle of Marion's finest preserves."

Sarah Miller rushed over to Uncle Jameson and handed him a jar, decorated with ribbon and a material topper. She turned to leave.

"Father," Raine said quickly, "may I be excused?"

Uncle Jameson nodded and set the preserves down on the table next to the last few slices of Emma's bread loaf.

Raine grabbed Sarah's hand and together they ran out of the kitchen toward the front of the house.

"Kissy, kissy, kissy," little Cole, the youngest of the Redbourne boys, called after them.

"Cole Redbourne," Leah chastised, "mind your manners, young man."

"Yes, ma'am. Sorry." He hung his head, but raised his eyes to look at his brothers across the table. Ethan and Rafe, the two just older than he, both nodded at him and he smiled.

Jonah found that he enjoyed the dynamics of the Redbourne family, so different from his own. He and his brothers had grown up without a mother, and had lived with a father who was always so distracted and focused on the ranch that they rarely ate their meals together, let alone spent time with him doing anything but work. He was grateful for the relationship he had with his brothers. They had always been close and had stuck together through it all.

Sitting here with the Redbournes was certainly a refreshing change and by the looks on Noah's and Lucas's faces, they felt the same way. Too bad Henry couldn't have been here to see it.

"Emma, I understand that you play," Leah said with a hand on her back. "Would you mind playing something for us?"

Emma shot an accusing look at Noah, who simply

shrugged his shoulders and smiled.

The whole family filed into the living area, except for the twins, who were left to clear the table and help Lottie with the dishes.

Jonah sat on the floor next to the fireplace. Cole and Ethan sat at his feet and Hannah climbed up onto his lap. He could get used to this.

Emma sat down at the beautiful piano sitting against the wall that separated the living area from the entryway. She stared at the empty music rack for a few moments before her fingers set down on top of the keys and the most beautiful melody stemmed from the instrument.

She continued to surprise him.

When Emma finished the elegant piece, she turned to see the smaller children gathered around the piano bench on the floor. Jonah enjoyed the light that came into her eyes at their attention.

"Let's see," she said, "if you'll recognize this one."

Her hands started jumping off the keys and immediately Hannah shot into the air and starting singing the lively song along with her. The others laughed. The song seemed familiar somehow, and the music grew louder with each new person who joined in.

"You are very talented, my dear," Leah told Emma when the spirited song concluded.

"Thank you. I really do love to play. I've missed it."

Jonah casually pulled himself up off the floor and sneaked outside for some fresh air. Memories of his childhood rushed into his mind. His mother had often gathered him and his brothers around the piano and they'd sung songs and picked at the keys for what had seemed like hours. He remembered his father smiling and laughing. He'd done that a lot. Until she left.

Jonah sat down on the steps and looked out over the vast

lands that made up the darkened horizon and leaned against the porch railing. He closed his eyes, listening.

He remembered all too well the fire that had consumed their mother's piano after their father had reduced the instrument to kindling with his axe. From that day on, music had been banned from the Deardon household.

It's time to let it go. To move on.

He'd held onto his grief, his anger toward his mother and resentment of his father, for way too long and it was stopping him from having a life worth living. He wanted a fresh start and marrying Emma was a step in the right direction.

The music stopped.

The front door opened. Jonah didn't need to turn around to know that Emma stood behind him. He could sense her somehow.

She sat down next to him. He didn't look at her at first. Didn't know what to say or where to begin.

"Is everything all right, Jonah?"

He liked it when she used his given name.

"The wedding is tomorrow," he said quietly.

Silence.

Emma slid her hand into his. Her touch sent a jolt up his arm.

"I've been thinking about that. I know you've lost a lot and I don't want to be the cause of any more sacrifices on your part. I'll sell you the land, Jonah. Grandfather's gone and over the last few days you've taught me that I can do hard things. I can learn how to take care of myself." She pulled her hand from his. "I release you of your family's obligation." Her eyes affixed to her hands, which were clasped now in a washing motion.

Jonah didn't know what he'd expected her to say, but that was not it. He looked at her and she met his eyes. In that moment, he realized why he'd become so protective of her.

Why he wanted nothing more than to be near her.

He loved her.

The revelation surprised him.

"Emma, I…" He pushed himself up from the stairs and strode a few feet into the yard.

"What is it? What's bothering you?" she asked, placing a hand on the back of his shoulder.

She'd followed him.

He spun around and without another thought, pulled her hard into him, capturing her lips with his, pleased when a soft moan vibrated in her throat. His arms encircled her completely and he pressed her more fully against him.

Her arms entwined around his neck and her fingers combed the hair at his nape before gripping it firmly with an attempt to pull him even closer. He groaned at her touch. No longer could he bear to think of letting her go, of allowing her to leave him. He wanted her. Needed her. He moved his hands beneath her arms—which dropped to his hips, her thumbs threading his belt loops—and he held her head firmly between his hands, his thumb running the length of her jaw and caressing her cheek. He drank in the sweet pleasure her lips allowed.

They parted ever so slightly and he rested his forehead against hers. When at last he pulled away enough to look into her face, her hair was slightly mussed and her mouth was swollen with desire.

"Finally," she whispered so softly he wasn't sure he'd heard her correctly.

How he wanted her.

Tomorrow, the voice in his head screamed at him.

He released her and took a step backward.

"The wedding is not until tomorrow, woman," he said fighting to catch his breath. "Please. Don't come any closer. I don't know if I have the strength to resist you much longer."

She stepped forward. She was playing with a fire he was sure she didn't understand.

"Stop." He put his hand up in a breathless warning.

"But I thought…"

It was too much. He closed the distance between them, placing a finger over her bewitching mouth, then took her hands in his and brought them up to his lips with a firm and aching kiss.

"Emma," he stared at her searching eyes, "obligation be damned. You are the most courageous and fascinating woman I have ever known. You are beautiful and smart and I *want* to be with you. Please marry me tomorrow. Be my wife. I want to build a life with you."

A single tear fell down Emma's passion flushed cheeks. "Finally," she said again with a smile. This time, there was no mistaking the word.

The hairs on Jonah's arms raised and he was hit with a sinking feeling. Something was wrong.

CHAPTER TWELVE

"Go inside," Jonah urged Emma. "Make sure everyone is okay."

She didn't stop to question him, but nodded and turned for the porch steps.

"And Emma?"

She turned and smiled at him.

"Will you ask Uncle Jameson and my brothers to come outside?"

The voices coming from the house, and the occasional giggle, were not unusual. But Jonah couldn't shake the ominous feeling that had settled in his gut. He reached for his gun. He'd left his belt and holster on the table next to the bed.

He spotted the woodpile where they'd put the broken planks of the fence they'd mended and wrapped his hand around one with a few nails still protruding from the end. The sun had fallen completely behind the hills now, but the moon was brighter than he'd seen it in a while.

He slowly made his way around the perimeter of the homestead.

Nothing.

You're going mad, Deardon.

Jonah had started back when he spotted Raine and Sarah sitting on the bench at the side of the house.

"Raine," he called.

"What? Huh?" The youth looked up. "Jonah? What are you doing?"

"Sorry to interrupt your sparking, but have you seen anything strange out here tonight?"

The girl, Sarah, giggled. "Raine, I best be gettin' home. Pa's going to be awfully worried."

"I can escort you home? It's dark out."

"That won't be necessary," a large man with a protruding belly and a thick moustache pulled up on a dark horse, a shotgun slung across his lap.

"Why, pa." Sarah stood up, appearing suddenly flustered and ran the length of the porch and skittered down the steps toward her father. "Goodbye, Raine," she said with a little wave and a smile before climbing up onto the horse behind her father.

"And Redbourne, you best remember not to keep my little girl past dark again, son."

"Yes, sir," Raine said sincerely. "You have my word."

Jonah breathed a sigh of relief. He needed to tune in better to his senses as he wasn't accustomed to false alarms.

Noah, Lucas, and Uncle Jameson joined them on the side of the house.

"What's wrong, Jonah?" Noah asked, a shotgun in hand. "Emma said you had a bad feeling."

Jonah looked at Raine.

"Mr. Miller just came to get Sarah," Raine explained, looking hard at his father. "With a shotgun."

Uncle Jameson shook his head. "You've got to be careful with him, son. Fathers can be—"

An ear-splitting scream came from the house.

They split up. Raine and Uncle Jameson headed to the back door, while Jonah and his brothers made for the front. Lucas handed him a pistol.

"Thought you might need this," he said quietly as he peeked through the window next to the door.

Jonah kept the nailed plank in his hand, but he took the gun as an extra precaution and gently reached for the doorknob. Click. It opened. Noah went in first, then Lucas, and Jonah brought up the rear.

Aunt Leah was visible from the living area, Hannah clutched in her arms. He couldn't see any of the other children because of the wall that separated them, but Aunt Leah was staring with concern up the stairs. Jonah couldn't see what or who she was looking at. He waved his brothers forward.

Where was Emma?

"Mr. Greeley?" Emma asked with an air of incredulity.

Jonah closed his eyes with relief.

"What are you doing here and why do you have my travelling case?"

Uncle Jameson appeared just around the kitchen doorway. Jonah could see him from his position, but doubted the intruder could.

"Miss Foster, please. I have travelled a long way to collect these documents. Please, just let me know. I don't want to hurt anyone." The man's voice was oily and high pitched.

Jonah figured he would have disliked the man anyhow.

"But I will," the man said, "if I have to. If I don't get these documents back to Mr. Horace, I'll be a dead man."

Uncle Jameson stepped out from behind the kitchen wall, his shotgun held firm in front of him. Raine had a rifle in his hands, cocked and ready when he walked two steps farther into the hallway.

Jonah nodded at his brothers who rounded one side of

the wall and at the same time he rounded the other.

A small man in a dark bowler hat stood on the stairs with Emma's old broken travelling case tucked up against his stomach, both arms holding it in front of him. The broken handle hung from the one bolt keeping it in place.

The man jumped at the sight of five armed men. His eyes darted back and forth between them and he gingerly took a step backward up the stairs.

Mr. Greeley, as Emma had called him, wore spectacles that had started to slide down his nose from the sweat that trickled down his face, and the small revolver he held dangled haphazardly from his fingers.

"How do you know this man, Emma?" Jonah asked without looking at her.

"He works for Mr. Horace, my grandfather's attorney."

"From Boston?"

"Yes," she whispered, "of course."

He redirected his attention to the intruder.

"What is so important about that old box that you would follow Miss Foster all the way from Boston?" Jonah inquired with a raised brow.

"I don't care about the case," the man spat, his features contorting from innocent victim to spurned culprit. "I just want the documents Horace gave her."

Her documents?

"You want our land?" Jonah asked incredulously.

Movement caught his eye from behind Mr. Greeley. The twins had somehow gotten up the stairs without the man knowing it.

"Of course not. What good would land in Oregon do for me, Mr. Deardon? Yes. I know who you are."

"It was you. In St. Joseph. You're the one who hired those boys to break into Millie's place."

"And if they'd done their job, it would have saved me a

lot of trouble. Luckily, Miss Millie knew where you all were headed, so I didn't have to follow too closely."

Levi quietly approached the top step. He had one of Lottie's heavy cast iron skillets in his hand. Tag knelt down and pulled something from his pocket and placed it on the top step.

A lizard.

With a little coaxing, the blue-green body strutted down the steps, effectively catching Mr. Greeley's attention and distracting him.

Levi stepped forward with the pan and knocked the man over the head with it. He immediately fell forward and tumbled down the remaining few steps.

"We got him," Levi said, clapping his brother on the back.

Aunt Leah and Emma both rushed forward to the man. He's still breathing. Aunt Leah let out a visible sigh of relief.

"Boys," Leah called, "help us get him on over to the couch."

"You're going to make him comfortable?" Uncle Jameson asked with disbelief.

"Levi and Tag, you two go get some rope from the barn. Your mother may give him something soft to sit on, but he's not going to be comfortable."

The boys snickered and ran down the stairs, jumping over the unconscious man's limp body, and out toward the barn.

Jonah stepped forward and pulled the travelling case from beneath the crumpled man.

"I want to see what was so damned important that he would risk breaking into a house full of people and men with guns."

"Raine, take Will and the two of you go collect the sheriff," Uncle Jameson directed. "Check the Miller's place.

I'm pretty sure he's visiting his folks tonight." He winked at his oldest son.

Jonah flipped the latches on the case and swung the lid upward. A worn yellow envelope had been tucked into the pouch at the back and Jonah pulled it free.

Inside, Foster's will was accompanied by the deed to the Oregon property and a very worn old photograph of a stern looking couple Jonah guessed to be Emma's parents. He picked up the deed over which the marriage agreement had been made to examine it. It seemed very thick and he realized there was another document hidden in its folds.

It was a property deed for a place called Orchard House in Boston, made out in Emma's name. Jonah continued to stare at the paper. If this Orchard House belonged to her, what would keep her from returning to Boston? What could he offer that would make her stay? She had already agreed to simply sell him the land in question, and if Orchard House was what he suspected, she would now be able to return home to her precious Boston.

He turned to look at Emma. Remembered how she had responded to his touch. To his kiss. He ached to pull her into his arms and know that she was his.

"What is it? Did you find something?" She walked up to him and casually placed her hand on his forearm.

He liked the feel of her touch and never wanted it to end. Despite how he felt for her, he had to tell her the truth, but at what cost?

"There is an extra deed in here," he told her.

"Of course, there is. Isn't that why we're here?"

"I mean, there's one for the Oregon spread and another for a place called Orchard House...in Boston. Both have your name on them."

Emma turned to look at him, her mouth slightly ajar and her eyes wide. She shook her head slightly and then backed up to lean against the overstuffed chair next to the couch.

"Impossible," she breathed. "I own Orchard House?"

"What is it?" he asked reluctantly.

"It's my home."

Home? How could he compete with that? He had to think fast. He could not lose her. Not when he'd only just found her.

"Do you know what this means?" Emma asked with a smile.

He didn't respond. Afraid to hear the answer.

CHAPTER THIRTEEN

Emma couldn't sleep. She tossed the quilt from her legs and sat up against the headboard of her bed. The night seemed unusually hot for October—even the thin nightshift she wore stuck to her skin.

Moonlight spilled into her room through a small slit in her curtains and she stood up to open them wide. She discovered there was no window there at all but a set of double doors that led out to a small veranda overlooking the field where the chairs and decorations had been set up for the wedding. She stood against the doorframe and allowed the light warm breeze to dance with the delicate material of her gown. It was beautiful here.

Emma could still hardly believe that Orchard House belonged to her. She knew God had a sense of humor, but this was ridiculous. After her grandfather's debts had been settled at his passing, Mr. Horace had assured her that following through on her grandfather's agreement with the Deardons was her only means of survival.

He'd obviously neglected to tell her that the house and everything left in it, still belonged to her. She chose to believe he'd simply made a mistake.

Emma didn't know what exactly was going on between her and Jonah, but she realized she wouldn't have met him if it hadn't been for that mistake. And if she hadn't have met him, she would never have experienced his impassioned kisses, never felt her heart leap through her chest when held her, never known what it meant to love him.

Orchard House was just that. A house. It had been her home for a long time. She'd grown up there. She'd had friends there. A life. It was familiar. And safe.

But now, so much had changed. She'd come so far. Learned so much. Returning to Boston would mean turning her back on a new life and everything she now held dear. It would mean turning her back on Jonah. She loved him, she had no doubt. But fear etched its ugly head into her thoughts.

He'd told her she was beautiful, that he wanted to make a life with her. What if he felt differently now that she was no longer impoverished with no place else to go, no other options? What if he expected her to return to her previous home and simply sell him the Oregon land as she'd proposed?

Emma had always wanted to marry for love. Was it too much to hope that she'd received exactly what she'd wished for? She hadn't realized until this moment how much she needed to hear the words. Needed to hear Jonah say he loved her. She didn't want to settle for a marriage of convenience. Now, she didn't have to.

A light flickered in the darkness. Emma peered over the veranda balustrade and spotted a lone figure sitting on the steps. Jonah's silhouette was unmistakable in the moonlight and she bit her lip at the thought of him. His kiss had seared into her memory. Unwittingly, she raised her fingers to her mouth and brushed them across her lips.

She needed sleep. Tomorrow promised to be a big day. Leah had agreed to take her into town in the morning. There was suddenly a lot to do.

"If you aren't going to marry her, Jonah, then I will."
Noah sat at the edge of his bunk and pulled on his boots.

"Like hell you will."

Noah laughed.

Jonah couldn't imagine the hell it would be to see Emma
with another man. "I can't very well marry her if she's going
back to Boston, now can I?"

"So, tell her not to go." Noah stood up and walked out
into the yard.

"It's not that simple." Jonah followed. Of course he
didn't want her to go, but he didn't want to be the woman's
second choice. He'd seen how well that had worked out for
his father.

"Why not? Have you told her you love her?"

Jonah stared at Noah. "How did y—"

Noah laughed. "I've known you a long time big brother
and I have never seen you quite so…alive as you are when
you're with her." Noah stopped and looked him square in the
face. "I also know you don't always let on how you're feeling.
Have you told her you love her?"

"No." He'd told her he wanted to be with her. Told her
she was beautiful, but he'd not said those specific words.

"Then, get to it."

Jonah didn't hesitate. Noah was right. She needed to
know and then he'd let her decision fall where it would.

He looked in the kitchen, by the pond, and even knocked
on her bedroom door, but he couldn't find Emma anywhere.

"Where is she?" he asked Lottie the moment she
emerged from the cellar. "Miss Foster. Where is she?"

"Señora Leah take her to town."

Town? She was leaving? He had to stop her.

Jonah carefully lifted the heavy box of food stuffs from

the family cook's arms and quickly carried it to the kitchen.

"Gracias," she called after him as he ran from the house to the stables.

Jonah was greeted with an empty stall. He'd let Perseus out into the fields last night to graze and run.

"Something wrong, Jonah?" Uncle Jameson strode into the stables with a sack of feed.

"What time does the stage pass through town on its way to St. Joseph?"

"You heading back?" Uncle Jameson set the feed on the floor next to the legs of the work table and pulled a knife from the sheath on his belt. "I thought we were going to have a wedding today."

"We are—God willing. If I can stop her from leaving."

Uncle Jameson stopped what he was doing at looked up at Jonah.

"The stage?" Jonah asked again.

Jameson pulled his watch from his pocket and clicked it open. "I reckon it'll be leaving Stone Creek within the next hour or so."

Jonah grabbed his bridle from the wall.

"Thanks." He ran to the pasture gate, and whistled—low and short.

"What are you doing, Jonah?" Little eight-year-old Cole stood next to him and looked out into the field.

"Bringing my bride home," Jonah said with a smile.

Cole looked up at him quizzically.

"She out in the field?"

"No."

"Then why are you still here?" Cole put the apple he'd been eating into his pocket, then placed two fingers at the corners of his mouth, curled his lip, and tried to whistle with one short blow. No sound came out.

Jonah laughed. "Don't worry, kid. You'll get it."

Where had his horse gotten off to?

He whistled one more time, hoping the horse would remember the call. They'd practiced a few times before leaving home, but it still needed some work. When he heard the familiar neigh of the chestnut gelding, Jonah turned to see his mount approaching from the other direction. He swung the gate wide and Perseus rode out into the yard and up to Jonah.

"Well done, boy!" he said, rubbing the mount enthusiastically on the nose.

"Whoa." Cole said with wide eyes. "Does he always come when you call him like that?"

"We're working on it," Jonah responded as he quickly strapped the bridle in place.

"Here, Perseus." Cole reached into his pocket and retrieved his apple, holding it out for the horse. "He deserves it."

"Yes, he does." Jonah pulled himself up bareback. "Will you go and tell Noah I've gone to town and I'll be back soon?"

Cole nodded. "I want to learn how to do that," Jonah heard the boy say as he turned for the bunkhouse.

Jonah smiled.

I have a stage to catch.

Jonah had been riding as hard as he'd dared for nearly three quarters of an hour. When he finally rode into Stone Creek, the dust from the stage hadn't yet settled.

He wasn't too late.

"We're almost there," he said, rubbing Perseus on his side. The back wheels of the stage peeked out from the cloud of dust that had turned up into the air as it departed from town and he urged his mount forward.

He had to dodge a woman and her child crossing the street, jump over a barrel of ale that had come loose from the supply wagon, and duck under a low hanging branch at the edge of town just past the saloon.

Jonah's heart was beating in rhythm with his horse's gait. He rehearsed in his mind one more time what he would say to her and hoped she would return the sentiments.

It's worth the risk.

It took a few minutes, but Jonah finally caught up to the stage. He sped up a little faster to get ahead of the burly driver.

"Stop," he yelled, swallowing a mouthful of dirt. He coughed and spit.

Let's try that again.

He rode up a little farther. "Stop!" ·

The man looked down at him hard and after a moment, he pulled on his reins and the stage came to a halt.

"I'm here for one of your passengers." Jonah flipped the man one of the silver coins he had in his pocket. "Thank you."

The driver caught the money and nodded, pulling thoughtfully on his long greying beard.

Jonah took a deep breath, dismounted, and stepped up onto the iron foot bar beneath the door.

"Miss Foster," he started as he looked inside.

Two very robust women, both in ridiculous hats looked at him and smiled awkwardly. He glanced at the other side of the coach to where a thin bearded man in a brown suit peered back at him with a look of utter annoyance.

Emma wasn't there.

"Uh, my mistake," he said and jumped down off the step.

It didn't make sense. He guessed it was possible that she'd hired a freighter or some other guide to take her to St.

Joseph. The only way he'd find out was to ride back into town and find Aunt Leah.

He pulled himself back up onto Perseus's back and called up to the driver.

"Carry on."

The driver shrugged his shoulders, picked up the reins to the four-horse team, and started moving again.

"I know you're tired, boy," Jonah whispered to Perseus. "But you can rest once we get back to town. I promise." He clicked his tongue and lifted the reins. "Let's go."

The short trip back to town only took a couple of minutes. Jonah pulled up in front of the livery and dismounted. He paid the stableman to brush, feed, and let Perseus rest a while. When he turned around, Aunt Leah walked out of the telegraph office with a smile, followed by a laughing Emma.

His heart lurched inside his chest. He caught her gaze and she smiled at him. If she'd have him, he'd be a very lucky man.

"Thank you, Leah. I couldn't have done this without you."

Emma and Leah had been to see the only attorney in Stone Creek to handle the matter of Orchard House. While Emma would always love Boston, she'd realized it was no longer her home.

"I think turning your old house into a boarding school for orphans is a wonderful idea," Leah said with a smile as they walked out of the telegraph office.

Emma had just sent Mr. Horace a notice of dismissal.

"Maybe I'll have to send some of my brood that direction."

Emma laughed.

They already sent a letter on the stage addressed to her friend Hattie, from the train, via Pony Express, in which Emma expressed her sincere desire to have the woman as headmistress of the new school. With the telegram to Mr. Horace, they had accomplished most everything on her list.

"We'd better be getting back. I'll expect our guests will start arriving at any time now and I'm afraid Jameson will not have any idea what to do with them."

Emma giggled and picked up the bottom of her skirt. Something caught her eye and she glanced up to see Jonah, standing in front of the livery.

When he caught her gaze, she smiled at him. He started purposefully toward her. Emma thought her heart might jump from her chest as the pounding grew stronger with each step he took. His hat rode low on his head and his shirt hugged the muscled flesh of his arms and chest. A look of utter determination set his jaw and he raised a single brow.

Jonah didn't say a word when he reached her. His hands delved into the tresses at her nape and he pulled her face upward to meet his ardent kiss. Her lips parted in eager response. A warm tingling tremor started in her belly and migrated downward until it reached her toes.

He moved his arms down around her waist, crushing her against him, and he lifted her from the ground, his lips still holding hers captive. Emma opened her palms against his back and slid them upward until they wrapped around his shoulders.

When he released her from their kiss, he didn't pull away.

"I love you Emma Foster," Jonah whispered.

He slid a hand down her arm until he found her hand. He squeezed and held out his other arm in the air.

"I love Emma Foster!" he shouted into the street as he turned with her in circles.

He pulled her back into him, clutching both hands to his chest.

"Marry me," he breathed. "Marry me today. Right now."

Emma giggled.

"We are getting married in just a few short hours, silly. Don't you remember? Redbourne Ranch? Aunt Leah?" Emma said as she motioned to Leah who stood in front of the buckboard with a grin stretching from ear to ear. "Guests should be starting to arrive about now."

"I thought I'd lost you." He slid his arms back down her arms and with both hands wrapped tightly around her waist, he placed his forehead against hers.

"Please don't ever do that to me again."

"What?"

"Leave."

"Why, Jonah Deardon, I love *you*. My home is wherever you are."

Jonah glanced up the row created between the two sections of chairs full of the townsfolk of Stone Creek. Emma stood there, dressed in the most elegant cream colored gown he had ever seen. Her hair was pulled back loosely, decorated with little sprigs of pale pink flowers, and her long raven tendrils cascaded down her shoulders in front of her.

Jonah stood up a little taller as she and Uncle Jameson made their way toward him, her hand tucked neatly in his arm.

She was beautiful.

"Are you sure you don't want *me* to marry her?" Noah whispered, his hand on Jonah's shoulder.

Jonah didn't respond. Couldn't. Looking at Emma took his breath away. He loved her, no question. He held out his hand for her to join him in front of the town reverend.

Uncle Jameson released Emma with a quick kiss on her cheek.

Emma slid her hand into Jonah's and met his eyes with a smile that warmed him from the inside. To think that just a few days ago he'd been devising ways to convince Emma Foster not to marry him. He'd been the idiot, not her.

"…to love, honor, and cherish from this day forward?"

Jonah brushed a stray lock of hair from Emma's face. Then he pried his eyes from away from hers long enough to see the preacher waiting expectantly for his response. He cleared his throat.

"I do." Jonah squeezed Emma's hand.

"Emma Foster, do you take Jonah Nicholas Deardon to be your lawfully wedded husband…to love, honor, and cherish from this day forward?"

Silence.

She met his eyes and smiled.

"Forever," she whispered with a nod. "I do."

"Forever," Jonah repeated.

"…I now pronounce you man and wife."

Jonah felt his smile stretch the width of his face as he and Emma turned to greet their guests.

"Well, kiss her already," Lucas shouted up at them.

Jonah looked down at Emma. The sun behind her cast a warm glow around her hair and face. Her cheeks had a touch of color, her eyes bright and smiling, and her lips looked full and inviting. She was indeed the most beautiful angel he'd ever seen.

"I love you, Mrs. Deardon."

"I love you, Mr. Deardon."

Jonah took her lips in his and knew that he was home.

WATCH FOR

the Blacksmith

REDBOURNE SERIES, BOOK THREE
ETHAN'S STORY

ABOUT THE AUTHOR

KELLI ANN MORGAN recognized a passion for writing at a very young age. Since that time, she has devoted herself to creativity of all sorts—moonlighting as a cover designer, photographer, jewelry designer, motivational speaker, and more.

Kelli Ann is a long-time member of the Romance Writers of America and was president of her local chapter in 2009. Her love of and talent for writing have opened many doors for her and she continues to look for new and exciting opportunities and calls to adventure. She feels very blessed to have a talented husband and son who inspire her on a consistent basis.

Her novels are on the sensual side of PG—without graphic love scenes. Great romance novels are those that make you feel the spectrum of emotion, that leave you wanting more, and it is her hope that every time you crack open one of her romance stories, that you walk away inspired, uplifted, and with a love of romance.

www.kelliannmorgan.com

Printed in Great Britain
by Amazon

53573821R00067